THE TREE OF THE TORAJA

PHILIPPE CLAUDEL

The Tree of the Toraja

Translated from the French by
Euan Cameron

MACLEHOSE PRESS
QUERCUS · LONDON

First published in the French language as *L'arbre du pays Toraja*
by Editions Stock, Paris, in 2016

First published in Great Britain in 2018 by MacLehose Press

MacLehose Press
An imprint of Quercus Publishing Ltd
Carmelite House
50 Victoria Embankment
London EC4Y 0DZ

An Hachette UK company

Copyright © Editions Stock 2016
English translation copyright © 2018 by Euan Cameron

"Gimme Shelter"
Written by Mick Jagger and Keith Richards.
Published by ABKCO Music, Inc. Used by permission. All rights reserved.

"Mysteries"
Words & Music by Beth Gibbons & Paul Webb
© Copyright 2002 Domino Publishing Company Limited/Chrysalis Music
Limited, a BMG Company. All Rights Reserved. International Copyright
Secured. Used by permission of Hal Leonard Europe Limited.

The moral right of Philippe Claudel to be identified
as the author of this work has been asserted in accordance with
the Copyright, Designs and Patents Act, 1988.

Euan Cameron asserts his moral right to be identified
as the translator of the work.

All rights reserved. No part of this publication may be reproduced or
transmitted in any form or by any means, electronic or mechanical, including
photocopy, recording, or any information storage and retrieval system,
without permission in writing from the publisher.

A CIP catalogue record for this book is available from the British Library.

ISBN (TPB) 978 0 85705 770 9
ISBN (Ebook) 978 0 85705 699 3

This book is a work of fiction. Names, characters, businesses,
organisations, places and events are either the product of the author's
imagination or are used fictitiously. Any resemblance to actual persons,
living or dead, events or locales is entirely coincidental.

2 4 6 8 10 9 7 5 3 1

Designed and typeset in Quadraat by Patty Rennie
Printed and bound in Denmark by Norhaven

God knows how I adore life

When the wind turns

On the shore lies another day

I cannot ask for more.

BETH GIBBONS

THE TREE OF THE TORAJA

I

ON THE ISLAND OF SULAWESI LIVE THE TORAJA. THE
existence of this race of people is punctuated obsessively by death.
When one of them dies, the arrangements for the funeral take up
weeks, months, sometimes years. It is the custom to invite all the
members of the dead person's family to the ceremony. This can
account for thousands of guests scattered over the whole of the
Indonesian archipelago, or even beyond. The cost of their travel,
and of accommodating and feeding them, is the responsibility of
family and friends. It is not unusual for them to fall into debt over a
long period in order to be able to maintain the tradition.

Wooden houses, delicate and graceful as small fishing boats, are
erected to house the guests. Livestock is bought in anticipation of
the banquets. Pigs and buffaloes will be sacrificed to accompany
the deceased. Throughout this time they preserve the corpse of this
person, who is not yet thought of as being dead, but as someone
who is sick – to masaki, in the language of the Toraja.

The burial place in which the body is interred is hewn out of the
rock of certain sacred cliffs. In the tombs, which are in the shape of

recessed cavities, lie the remains of other members of the same family, watched over by wooden idols. Occasionally, the sarcophagi rot and split open. The bones then fall to the ground and are left there, among the leaves and the earth.

I travelled across the land of the Toraja during the spring of 2012. In this island that was hitherto unknown to me I rediscovered what I have always loved elsewhere in Indonesia: the people, smiling and peaceful; the scenery, undulating, sometimes steep, that is made up of infinite shades of green, from the palest to the most muted; the skies, which can be wide and blue and become almost perpendicular by the following day, a collage of high, leaden clouds that suddenly burst and release a warm rain that falls over the forests, paths and rice fields; the night, which comes early, very suddenly, and sets up the clamour of insects and geckoes; the pleasure of drinking an iced beer while eating a nasi goreng or satays of goat's meat while sitting on a pavement, on plastic chairs designed for dwarfs; of smoking a kretek smelling of nutmeg and cinnamon.

In a clearing, close to a village in Toraja, I was shown a particular tree. Striking and majestic, it rose from the forest a few hundred metres below the houses. It is a burial place set aside for very young children who have died during their early months. A cavity is carved out of the trunk of the tree. The little corpse wrapped in a shroud is placed inside. The opening of the sylvan tomb is filled in with a weave of branches and cloths. Gradually, over the course of years, the wood of the tree grows over it, retaining the child's body within its own large body, beneath its newly healed bark. Then, very slowly, in harmony with the patient rhythm of the tree's growth, begins the journey that will see it rise up towards the heavens.

We bury our dead. We burn them too. Never would we dream of entrusting them to the trees. Yet we lack neither forests nor imagination. Our beliefs, however, have grown meaningless and inconsequential. We perpetuate rituals that most of us would find very hard to explain. In our world, nowadays, we play down the presence of death. The people of Toraja make it the focal point of theirs. So which of us is on the right path?

That same evening, drinking beer and smoking *kreteks* on the little balcony of my hotel room, I thought again of the tree and of its wood nourished with delicate bones and dead flesh. Some elderly American ladies were laughing very loudly down below, finishing their dinner on the terrace of the restaurant. I had come across them on my way back to the hotel. They were wearing pink trainers and were dressed in khaki hiking slacks with numerous pockets, cotton blouses and the sort of waistcoats worn by front-line correspondents. Their heads were adorned with hair that was white or mauve, occasionally deep purple. They all had the same reconstructed noses, the same stretched-apart eyes, the same newly fleshed-out lips. They had reached the final stage of their lives, but their faces had the abstracted and simplistic aspect of young girls, artificial and identical-looking. You might have thought they were dolls that had escaped from some sort of shop selling hideous paraphernalia for goodness knows what type of customer. I thought of all the useless artifices we apply to our bodies to elude time and our fears.

Opposite me, in the Indonesian night, as I was enjoying the scent of the cigarettes, I could make out the clear outlines of the buffaloes, standing dozing in the midst of the rice fields, their bent heads lowered towards the mud. A fine rain as well as a little mist seeped down their motionless bodies. They seemed to belong to a different century. I could sense them fading away. I thought of death. Of the advent of life. Of the faltering dance, sometimes beautiful, sometimes grotesque, that is our life. Of our end too. Toads were chattering. Large bats were hovering above my head in a silent duel. Three months ago, I had just reached the age of fifty. Did that signify anything?

Beside me, as always, there lay a book. That evening it was *The Ghost Rider* by Ismaïl Kadaré, which I reread at least once every two years. It is a very beautiful story about promises, death, phantoms and riding horses. About winter, too, which is the season during which I have always thought I become truly myself. I had a notebook and a fountain pen that I bought more than ten years ago in a market in Saigon. I no longer remember whether I took notes as I thought of the tree and its bark enveloping the small invisible bodies. I can't be sure: sometimes one writes better in one's head than anywhere else. I was between two films, in that difficult place where you question yourself about what you do, pondering whether it is worthwhile, whether it has any point. And where you are even less sure whether you should continue.

My last full-length film had had a poor reception. The public had not rushed to see it. It had fared slightly better abroad, in the dozen or so countries in which it had been shown and to which I had travelled too, replying to the same questions, producing the same smile for photographers, and finding myself alone in the evening in my hotel room gazing at the miniatures in the mini-bar as if they shared my misfortune. After the tour, I had decided to forget this film that had consumed two years of my life, to turn over a new leaf within myself, and I set off for Sulawesi with a renewed longing for images, as yet vague and hazy, that were beginning to dawn on me and were awaiting a clarification that I was in no hurry to take on. For a long time, I have understood that we do not make films, but that they come from within us and emerge when they intend to do so, at the moment that they have chosen.

The elderly Americans – it is as though I was talking about cars – had quietened down. They had probably returned to their bedrooms. I imagined them now alone, standing in front of their bathroom mirrors, each of them peering at her artificial face and sadly recognising her true age. Every illusion contains its bitter destruction.

Three days later I was back in France. As soon as I got into my apartment, I lay down my luggage and drank a glass of tap water as I looked around. I felt as though I had arrived in a foreign country. The smells were certainly recognisable, but they belonged to city life, which I had been away from and where I had not yet found my bearings. The floorboards creaked beneath my feet. Dead flies, their legs turned towards the ceiling, had managed to expire collectively on the windowsills. I still felt both normal and exotic. I still had the peculiar taste of *kreteks* in my mouth.

I could hear some familiar sounds above me, however, in particular the out-of-tune piano that belonged to Monsieur Bellagar, my elderly, half-blind neighbour on the eighth floor, whose features and elegant neckties were somewhat reminiscent of Jorge Luis Borges, and who played tunes from Central Europe in a melancholy manner for hours on end.

I walked around the rooms, which can be done very quickly since there are only three of them, and I listened to the messages that had accrued on my answering machine, which was blinking on a low table in the sitting room, beside the photograph of Florence, my former wife, who was smiling at me. Among them I came across one from Eugène.

"You're going to laugh," he told me. "I've got a nasty cancer."

II

I DID NOT ACTUALLY LAUGH, BUT I DO ADMIT TO having smiled. Out of sorrow, no doubt. Or rather sadness. Out of annoyance. The smile of a chess-player defeated by someone stronger than him. Death has been circling around me for several years. She is trying to fence me in. To draw as close as possible to me. In order to sound me out a little. To make me realise that I am getting older? That I must expect her? That the match has begun even though I am not yet aware that I've been called from the changing room? Perhaps.

In one of my numerous notebooks in which jottings accumulate that I never read, I remember having stuck a small reproduction of a Dürer engraving: it depicts a couple of young lovers embracing, and behind them, a few metres away and half-concealed by a tree, Death is watching them. The portrayal is instructive, a skeleton, a scythe, and the simple message: all beauty blossoms in the shadow of the ultimate peril. We forget our fleeting condition and our lives take place beneath the gaze of the one who will not forget us. Should we in that case assimilate death into the course of our lives as the Toraja people perhaps do? Do they live more sensibly than us?

I have always been haunted by the words of Montaigne that "to philosophise is to learn how to die" and that "it is not death that is difficult but dying". I am not a sixteenth-century man, accustomed to epidemics, to wars, to the sudden and frequent loss of friends, parents and children, and for whom a forty-year-old is already an old man. But the books we read affect us with the intensity of a knife thrust into an organ without the "survival prognosis" – this is an expression that has always delighted me in that it associates a light-hearted subject, such as a horoscope, a racegoer's prediction, a weather forecast, with a word that causes us to tremble like a leaf – being really life-threatening. Besides, if one is in good health, when does this so-called prognosis, without our knowing anything about it, start being "life-threatening"? Speaking about someone in this way makes one think of a sailor waiting for his ship on the quayside.

I'm not afraid of anything as far as I personally am concerned. I don't fear what I do not know, quite the reverse no doubt of early human beings at the dawn of mankind for whom horror derived only from what was unknown. Living at the beginning of the third millennium, I know only too well how much the composition of my environment conceals lethal forces. We have made our earth into a toxic old hotchpotch and our commercial companies with their spotless shop windows are large, hidden dumping grounds, crammed with countless poisons and explosive charges. No, my fear does not stem from a lack of knowledge, but rather a surplus, and of course I dread the deaths of those who are close to me rather more than my own, which is not, as one might suppose, the opposite of selfishness, but its highest form.

I rang Eugène and he answered immediately. His voice was cheerful. Normal. He tried to make me talk about my journey and I tried to make him talk about his cancer. It was a dialogue of the deaf, which we quickly concluded with the promise that we would dine together that same evening.

My suitcase still stood at the entrance to the apartment. The image suddenly struck me. An onlooker, on coming across it, would have been incapable of telling whether it indicated an arrival or a departure. This made me think that if we are sometimes unable to discover the truth about simple questions such as this, how can we claim to know the truth about more opaque mysteries?

In the shower, I thought about Eugène. About how I would look at him or greet him. Should I appear concerned straight away or more reassuring? Light-hearted or solemn? Should I confront the subject head on or let him take the initiative? The burning water flowed over my shoulders. I stood there for ten minutes, and I still didn't know how I was going to treat him. I felt ridiculous all of a sudden. Why should I need to prepare for our reunion? It wasn't a job interview, or an oral examination. I realised how much what he had revealed to me had begun to alter the situation. The fact that he had told me he had been diagnosed with cancer had managed to modify my sense of apprehension about him; it was as though, now that he was afflicted with this disease, he was not quite the man I had known, but was becoming a somewhat strange creature with whom I still did not know how I should behave.

In our society, the word "cancer" resonates as though it were an anteroom of death. People are never cured of cancer. At best, they are "in remission" – does the remission of sins bear any similarity? An unpleasant disease that nevertheless has a pretty name, although many obituaries and announcements of deaths prefer to conceal it behind circumlocutions that usually refer to "long illnesses". Often this is untrue, in fact, for there are cancers that can be very quick, that destroy bodies in a few months, even in a few weeks, anxious as they are no doubt to attack other bodies. The patients are numerous. They never peter out.

I have also noticed that for some years we no longer talk about "cancerologists" when alluding to specialists in the disease, but about "oncologists". The word is less specific, more muted in its resonance and possibly reassuring. I don't know why I associate it with seafood, with fishing on foot in June from a beach in Brittany, the weather slightly chilly, with sharp aromas of iodine and seaweed. Yes, an oncologist for me is a lonely, retired person, perhaps a widower, who makes use of his now constant spare time to roam around the sandy expanses at low tide, wearing yellow rubber boots, prodding in ponds and crevices in the rocks in search of fish that may be trapped there, and scraping stones to which mussels, whelks and sea urchins cling like families of refugees. Oncologist: a word for crossword addicts or television games enthusiasts.

Eugène and I laughed a great deal over dinner. A little too much.

And we drank too much as well. Especially me. Bordeaux wines, of course, since Eugène only likes red Bordeaux, although that evening, on my way home, I remembered that he had scarcely touched his glass.

We had met in our favourite brasserie, the one we have been going to for years, in the 9th arrondissement. I like the rather slow pace of life there. We have "our" table. The waiters, of whom there are three, Michel, Gérard and Jean, know us and call us by our first names, but they use the more respectful *vous* form of address. They look like brasserie waiters, who, as we know, are the aristocrats of the profession: tall, with moustaches, paunches, large white aprons, black bow-ties. They know how to prepare a tartare sauce to perfection, how to fillet a sole, how to *flamber* kidneys or crêpes Suzette. All somewhat reminiscent of Claude Sautet's 1983 film "*Garçon!*". I'm always delighted when life resembles cinema.

Eugène ordered calves' liver and I chose an andouillette. We shared a poireaux vinaigrette beforehand and a millefeuille for dessert. Two coffees. The bill. This was Eugène's, who only ever allows himself to be invited out once a year, on his birthday, May 28.

I kept the packet of *kreteks* that I wanted to give to him in my pocket throughout dinner. I left with it. As I did with everything that I had wanted to tell him about the people of Toraja, the funeral rites, the children's tree. Eugène arrived after me. I had been sitting at the wall-seat for ten minutes. Gérard had brought me a glass of white Rully and complimented me on how well I looked. The revolving door began to turn. Eugène appeared. The same as ever, his features glowing. The inevitable jeans. The inevitable blue blazer. White shirt. Brown moccasins. Looking like a teenager. Thick pepper-and-salt hair. I got to my feet. We embraced and hugged one another, possibly a longer hug than usual. Without doing so deliberately, I think I was the one who prolonged the clasp.

Eugène is my producer and my best friend. He was my producer originally; then, gradually, he became my best friend. I don't know whether I am his. I prefer not to ponder such matters. We never truly know what we mean to other people and some of my greatest sorrows have been due to this type of disillusionment.

I told him about Sulawesi, the skies, the roads built of red earth, the forests haunted by the cries of monkeys, the after-dark markets, the lovely smell of the braziers on which the meat is cooked, the immense stillness reflected on the lakes, the elderly American women with their mauve hair, the little boy who had come towards me as I was walking along the thin ridge separating two paddy fields bristling with stalks of rice, and who had offered me his hand. I was moved and I had grasped it, thinking that he needed my encouragement and help to make his way, whereas in fact, I realised a little later, it was he who, imagining me to be very old, thought that he could help prevent me from falling over.

It was just when the millefeuille arrived that I dared take the plunge. Eugène had not mentioned the subject throughout dinner. He seemed so happy. He seemed so much as he always had been that I wondered whether I hadn't dreamed about the message on the answering machine.

"When I said 'nasty', it was to alarm you. There's nothing nasty about it. It's an ordinary cancer, a novice what's more. Probably a mere amateur. Everything has been caught in time. A small patch on the left lung. I've seen the top specialists. Ninon has taken care of everything. A short operation followed by a light course of chemo, and we won't mention it again."

Ninon is Eugène's eldest daughter. She is a psychiatrist. She has just set up her own practice. Eugène has five children. By five different wives. The youngest is not yet six years old. "I had some of them for you," he often says to me. Eugène falls in love frequently. And whenever Eugène is in love, he produces a child.

Eugène said nothing. He smiled at me. He speared a bit of mille-feuille with his fork, closed his eyes as he savoured it, and then said to me, pointing at the patisserie:

"God exists, you know. There's no doubt about it."

Then he raised his glass and we drank a toast, to God, to the millefeuille, to ourselves, to life.

Eugène died less than six months later, on February 23, 2013. His cancer really was nasty and within a few months it grew steadily worse. It was not a novice as he had believed, but an old professional which had done its work methodically. A ruthless hired killer. In the week preceding his death, during the daily visits I made to the palliative care department of the hospital, I finally told him about the tree of the Toraja. Morphine had helped relax his face, swollen by successive courses of treatment. He no longer had a single hair on his head. An Italian actor whom he was very fond of had given him a gardener's hat made of woven straw, which he never took off. He called his bed on wheels "his wheelbarrow". He listened to me with half-closed eyes, a smile on his lips. I placed the packet of *kreteks* on his bedside table. I kissed his cheeks, which for several weeks had felt constantly cold, like marble. He drew me to him with his hand and whispered in my ear:

"Death makes children of us all."

Since I looked somewhat puzzled, he added: "I'm telling you this for your tree."

These were the last words I heard him utter.

The following day he fell into a brief coma from which he never emerged.

III

I AM AWARE THAT I JUMBLE UP TENSES AS I WRITE, THE past historic, the present, the perfect and the imperfect; and the rules of normal narrative do not allow cohabitation. When I make films, I do not bother about such matters. I let the shots slip by one by one, without ever resorting to flashbacks any more than I do to leaps forward. Very early on, the cinema seemed to me to be an art that was focused on the future: on the future of characters, of situations, of settings, of clouds driven by the wind. I have always considered that surgery performed on time – apart from ellipses which, after all, are merely compressions, the removal of empty spaces for the sake of the drama in which, paradoxically, by cutting time one creates it – was immoral (I sometimes use big words). And I don't think a film director should avail himself of this right, one that no human being possesses, even though many dream of doing so: to be able to revisit lost moments of the past, or to experience in advance what the future may be.

Literature, on the other hand, is a kid goat that wears no halter. It can do everything and it is the freest of arts. Eugène had given me

The Invention of Morel by Adolfo Bioy Casares. "You'll like this." I did like it. Eugène was a producer who read books. Not many of them do. He had the ability to put me on the right track by passing on books when I was working on a subject, even though the stories and novels that he referred me to did not, on a first reading, appear to have any direct link with the film that I was trying to write.

The celebrated invention in the novel by this Argentine writer consists of a machine that allows one to record moments from life and to replay them identically, just as easily as one might play a record. The hero has thus found the means of liberating himself from time, retrieving certain episodes from time's inexorable course that were destined for the destruction it reaps on everything, as Ovid wrote more than two thousand years ago.

The script that I was working on at the time had its basis in an autobiographical event: the suicide of a friend from my youth, Jean-Christophe, who took his own life at the age of nineteen, unable to bear the fact that the girl he loved did not love him. Even today, when I call him to mind, his features return to my memory with the utmost clarity, whereas I have trouble recalling the faces of certain of my acquaintances when I haven't been in touch with them for a few months.

Jean-Christophe was not exactly a close friend, but for six years we had shared the same humdrum daily routine at a provincial boarding school in Lorraine, twenty or so kilometres from the small town where I was born. My mother had sent me there because of the quality of the teaching. She hoped I would have a career that would take me out of the rustic, working-class milieu in which our family had lived for centuries. In this respect, she gambled wisely.

I remember that Jean-Christophe smoked Gitanes. He had started early. In Year 3, I believe. Winter and summer, he only ever wore a plain white shirt, open to the chest. He never seemed to feel the cold. His eyes were always gazing into the distance. Beyond the face of the person he was talking to. Beyond the face of the teacher who was asking questions. Beyond the horizon, whenever we went for walks on Wednesday afternoons. Beyond time itself perhaps.

The last occasion that I spoke to Jean-Christophe was during the night, in the shower room adjoining our dormitory. A few of us used to meet to discuss philosophy, or music, and to smoke cigarettes out of the window in the dark. We were in our final year. I can't recall what it was about, but that night I had an argument with him. I remember I made some harsh remarks about him and that I tried to humiliate him by using words more fluently than my classmate, whose slightly thick lips never seemed to be able to detach themselves quite from the words they were pronouncing.

It was towards the end of the school year. The baccalauréat exams began a few days later. We never spoke to one another again. After the night's altercation, I felt embarrassed and ashamed of myself, but I did nothing to let him know this. We left the lycée and each of us tried to make our first steps in a life in which the other no longer featured. I did not miss him, and I think I can truthfully say that he would not have missed me either. A year later, a girl we both knew whom I bumped into in a street in Nancy where I had enrolled at the university, informed me that Jean-Christophe had committed suicide.

I don't know whether the reason the memory of his death remains with me – with a steadfastness, a sorrow and a clarity that do not diminish – is because I could not forgive myself for hurting him, or because his final act was also entirely pointless. The girl for whom he had killed himself never knew. To say that she was not worth it is self-evident. And I'm not talking of her personal qualities, but of the link between her existence on this earth and the ending of the life of someone from this same earth that she had unwittingly brought about.

At the end of "Swann in Love" in the first volume of *In Search of Lost Time*, Proust has Swann say about Odette: "To think that I've wasted years of my life, that I've longed to die, that I've experienced my greatest love, for a woman who didn't appeal to me, who wasn't even my type!" I've never been able to read these lines without thinking of Jean-Christophe, without seeing his vacant and faraway expression, his fingers curled around his cigarette, his white and scrawny figure in the school playground battered by the winter gale, and the shower room in which our quarrel occurred. Furthermore, I believe that when I left the room that night, Jean-Christophe's eyes were also a little moist, and my heart concurred with the definition that Pascal gives of men's hearts that I read later on: it was "hollow and full of filth".

For a long time I wondered how I could express this in a film, both the memory of my friend, or rather the significance of this memory, and the way in which it has somehow shaped my life, and Swann's disillusioned comment, a Swann who observed the waste, but a Swann who was alive, who chose life and rejected the temptation of death.

Remorse, time, death and memory are merely different masks for an experience that has no name in the language, and that at its simplest could be described by the expression "life's uses". When one thinks of it, the whole of our existence is based on the experiments we make with it. Faced with the passage of time, we never stop manufacturing stratagems, machines, feelings, delusions to try to make light of it, to deceive it, to overtake it, to expand or accelerate it, to suspend it or to dissolve it like a sugar lump at the bottom of a cup.

Eugène had listened to me, feet on his desk, as he drank tea and puffed at one of the untipped Craven As that he chain-smoked. Sometimes our sessions lasted for hours. One of us listened to the other. There was little actual conversation. I think we needed several days and a few nights without seeing each other for the words of one to prompt responses from the other, which he pronounced on during the following session. And this was our usual pattern of work. It was a few days after I had mentioned Jean-Christophe's suicide that Eugène gave me *The Invention of Morel*.

"You'll like this."

The film was called *"Pas mon genre"* ("Not My Type"). I shot it with Portuguese actors, entirely in Lisbon, which is a hypnotic and extremely human city. Oddly enough, the French surrealists have not celebrated it much. Yet it seems to me that if the world possesses the power to turn itself inside out like a glove in certain places, then Lisbon certainly shares that elective geography, full of passageways, two-way corridors, cities within cities, built of silky white stone. I think I could say much the same about Montevideo, which I discovered later on, and also Valparaiso.

We were at the very beginning of the year 2000. It was a delightful shoot, with a small team and some marvellous actors. Eugène often came to see us. He would arrive on Thursday evening on the last flight and leave again on Monday morning. He was in love that year. Her name was Angelina. She worked for a shoemaker. An Italian girl with a flowery accent. It didn't last long. Not long enough for him to give her a child. It was a very mild summer. Or rather, a late summer. We spent our evenings drinking vinho verde in the neighbourhood cafés of the Bairro Alto, nibbling at plump violet olives and eating sardines that had been cooked on grills in small yards where the walls were covered in *azulejo* tiles.

I was still married in those days. Florence had snuggled up close to me, a grey shawl thrown around her shoulders. We were listening to Eugène and felt happy with life. There were stars in the sky that were like eyes gazing at us. We were staying in an apartment reminiscent of a huge monastic cell, with whitewashed walls and uneven flooring that consisted of hexagonal earthenware paving stones the colour of lava.

A character in the film was called Jean-Christophe. He was certainly not a young man, but on the contrary an elderly man who kept an antiquarian bookshop. With my costume supervisor I arranged for him to be dressed in clothes that my school friend would have worn, a white shirt open wide at the neck that displayed a mottled chest covered with fine grey hairs, and black canvas trousers. Jean-Christophe had grown old. Thanks to me. Thanks to the cinema. He read Proust and recounted Morel's story to a young woman who did not know she was loved by a young man whom she walked past every day on her way to work.

"*Pas mon genre*" is a film about parallel routes, the corridors of time. In it, people meet each other a great deal. They rarely embrace one another. The city and the ocean serve as endless reference points for fleeting exchanges. The characters become attached to certain places but they have the calm, elegant beauty of those who are indifferent. No one dies in this film, but everything gradually vanishes. Apart from the city.

For Eugène and me it was our greatest popular hit, a claim that must be qualified immediately for we never had genuine successes. Let's just say that "*Pas mon genre*" was not a failure, and that it managed to appeal to a certain category of women and men who, like ourselves no doubt, cared about time and life, about the ups and the downs, about faces that drift by and fade away, about voices that resonate and painful memories that never manage to be assuaged or to grow dim.

IV

WHEN EUGÈNE TOLD ME ABOUT HIS ILLNESS, THE ONLY experience I had had of the death of anyone close to me was that of my father who, four years earlier, had been found by his bed, his life having ended one summer morning at dawn, bowed down beneath the weight of his eighty-nine years, as well as the deaths, longer ago, of fellow mountain climbers. The latter, tragic and violent, had happened to young people, in full possession of their physical capabilities. Their accidental deaths were the result of a passion for altitude and taking risks, two attributes that the great majority of people never come up against. For me, climbing was an intense passion, one of which I am still struggling to cure myself, even though my slowly ageing body restores me to reason and moderation year after year.

I don't know why this excessive love of climbing and scaling peaks began to take root in adolescence. No-one in my family was interested in any sport and we could never take holidays, because we could not afford them. The province of Lorraine consists mainly of rural landscapes, and even though the Vosges are mountains, erosion has reduced them to rounded tops and modest altitudes. Here again, it seems to me that it was literature and the cinema that revealed to me what I had not been allowed to see at the time. And I owe both my craving and its gratification to the novels of Frison-Roche, to books by Samivel and by Gaston Rébuffat; to German films of the interwar period such as "The Blue Light" in which Leni Riefenstahl, the actress and film director, seems to be possessed by the exhilaration of emptiness and physical endurance that I had never experienced, to those of Marcel Ichac, René Vernadet, Gérard Herzog, and many others; to obscure documentaries of Himalayan expeditions filmed in 16mm by numbed hands in which creatures covered by many layers of down, their eyes disappearing behind goggles, advance step by step, bent against the wind, over an endless ridge of snow, as though their aim was to walk a little further and eventually to walk on the sky itself.

Mountain climbing is not merely a sport, it is a desire to measure the disparity of proportions, those of space as well as those of time. The man who climbs is faced with elements which, compared to his size and his life expectancy, represent an insignificant quantity, one so infinitesimal that it would be dismissed in their calculations by the most scrupulous of mathematicians. Down below, or up there, we are nothing. And the efforts to which we go to give the illusion that for a brief moment we are the overlords, on the pretext that we have managed to plot a course and conquer a peak, are of no consequence to the great masses of ice and stone amongst which our bodies suffer, our fingers are grazed, our lips crack and our eyes burn.

Mountain climbing is a harsh lesson in philosophy. But in the feeling that seizes hold of those who finally reach the top of the route they have mapped out, and who contemplate at their feet the world from which they have come and to which they must all too soon descend once more, there is also a joy that is unalloyed and unblemished. It has always seemed to me that in these strictly speaking inhuman territories, those human feelings that sustain and justify our lives can be tested to the highest degree, miraculously shorn of the crude imperfections with which the world burdens them.

This explains the gamble with danger and sometimes with death. Yet it is never the latter that the climber seeks in the mountains. For him it is more a question of delving as far as possible into this experience of pure feelings that I have just described, of achieving their perfection, their quintessence, and savouring the lightheadedness that comes over us when we rediscover them, which is increased by the exhaustion that twists, kneads and divinely mauls every muscle of our body like the rough, strong hand of a masseur. When I tried to explain this to Eugène, he cloaked himself in the smoke of his Craven A and smiled at me mockingly.

I can see once more the faces of Marco, Alain, Tipol, Nicolas, Chloé and the two Patricks. All of them died on mountains, in the Alps, the Andes, the Karakorum, the Annapurna circuit, on Spitzbergen. I can see them alive, in the final moments before departure, young and soon to die, drinking beer on the terraces of Chamonix cafés where we sprawled, stinking unwashed climbers, watching the boys and girls go by, the pretty girls of countless summers, who looked at us too, dirty and sunburnt as we were, scorched by the highest of suns, that of the gods and of space.

I learned of their deaths through a telephone call, a telegram from a friend, a brief comment in a newspaper. They were always faraway deaths, disconnected from my life, even though I sometimes knew the place where they had died and could imagine their vast tomb, beaten by the winds, falling stones, seracs and avalanches. For me, they were not entirely dead. They were no longer alive. It was not the same thing.

Then there was Gary, and that was different. I spent three nights sleeping beside his corpse. Sleeping is not the right word. I scarcely closed my eyes. Whereas Gary kept his wide open. I was not able to close them for him. Bad weather had caught us unawares on our descent from the Dames Anglaises, two granite sentinels that bisect the elegant Peuterey ridge that runs along the Italian side of the border as far as the summit of Mont Blanc, and whose vast outline of dark rock and lacy snow can be seen from Courmayeur.

We were both twenty-eight. We had been climbing together for six years already. We were roped to one another, by which I mean we formed an entity that does not exist beyond the world of climbing: a couple of human beings each of whom blindly and at every moment places his life in the hands of the other person. The storm came swooping down on us with unforeseeable speed. Ever since we had woken up in our bivouac, we had been aware that it was certainly a little too hot for the season at this altitude – it was mid-June – but we had taken no notice. A few clouds – inoffensive and slow-moving stratus – had begun to cast a dirty, milky trace over the sky, then towards the Grandes Jorasses, from Switzerland, came low, dark, swollen rolls of them like immense varicose veins, driven by a silent wind that tore across the blue sky like the muddy waves of a spring tide along the shore.

Gary was abseiling down the final section when I heard bees buzzing around me, as we climbers refer to the acoustic phenomenon of static electricity, and noticed bluish and yellow sparks coming from the tip of my ice-axe and the bunch of cams and pitons that dangled from my harness. When I looked up to warn Gary, he was still abseiling down and spiralling beneath an overhang. He was singing at the top of his voice. A Rolling Stones number: "Gimme Shelter". But the wind was already blowing away the words and driving the clouds towards him that blotted out the top of the Dames.

The flash of lightning, orange and zigzagging, shot out suddenly from the grey mass and, I believe, struck my friend at chest height. He let go of the rope and his freed descender caused him to shoot downwards like a bag of loose clothing. The retaining knots that I always make at the bottom of the two abseil ropes stopped him abruptly, a metre away from me. The elasticity of the rope caused him to rebound briefly, like a puppet, before he gradually came to a standstill, his arms hanging alongside his inert body, his head toppling over his right shoulder. Blood trickled from both his ears. His lips moved. He was mumbling something that I was unable to understand. His eyes were fixed on a distant point, behind me. I freed him from the rope and attached him to the belay as quickly as I could, and I laid him on the small ledge where there was room for both of us. Two more flashes of lightning struck and thunderclaps reverberated close to us, causing pieces of rock to scatter into space. A stench of wet dust and gravel rose up from far below. Then the storm moved angrily on. The mist hid the landscape from us. The temperature plummeted, and the first snowflakes soon began to flutter around us.

> *Ooh, a storm is threatening*
> *My very life today*
> *If I don't get some shelter*
> *Ooh yeah, I'm gonna fade away.*

Gary was singing softly to himself. My friend was departing his life to a Rolling Stones song. I had settled him closely against me and covered him with his anorak and the canvas from our tent. I had removed his helmet and slipped his balaclava on over his head and I put a pair of silk gloves on his hands and his thick woollen mittens. It was snowing heavily. The blood continued to seep from his ears. A thin, uninterrupted flow that dried quickly upon his neck and on the edge of his balaclava, staining it with trickles of dark blood. He did not answer any of my questions or respond to any of my promptings.

He appeared neither to see me nor to hear me. He did not seem to be in any pain. His face was calm. From time to time I thought I saw the glimmer of a smile. I brushed away the snowflakes that were insolently settling on him. I held his hands. I tried to make him drink what was left in the thermos, but the tea ran down the sides of his lips that continued to murmur:

> *Gimme, gimme shelter*
> *Or I'm gonna fade away*
> *Or I'm gonna fade away*
> *Or I'm gonna fade away.*

The first night came.
Endless. It seemed like a thousand nights.
The following morning, Gary had stopped singing.
Then there were the two following nights.
And then all the others.
All those others that are my life.

> *Or I'm gonna fade away*
> *Fade away, fade away . . .*

In the drawer of my bedside table, I have the last photograph that I took of Gary, only a few hours before the accident. He is on the summit of the Noire de Peuterey. He is smiling. He is looking at me. He is twenty-eight years old. He radiates the exuberance and beauty of youth. He does not know yet that he is preparing to withdraw from Time. I often pick up the photograph. I look at him as though I were there with him. I smile back at him. Or I may be smiling at myself, a distant self who is no longer there.

It was years before I felt able to tell Eugène about what happened to Gary, constrained by the fear of betraying a dead friend by confiding in one who was alive. And one day I told him everything. It was winter. It was snowing outside. One snowfall recalled another. Eugène smoked his Craven A as he listened to me.

A few days later, he gave me a copy of *Ascension* by Ludwig Hohl, a limpid account of mountains and friendship.

"You'll like this."

V

WE WHO LIVE ON ARE ENVELOPED BY THE WHISPERS OF our ghosts. Our flesh and the make-up of our beings are the result of molecular combinations and a complex weaving of words, images, feelings, moments, smells and scenes that are linked with those women and men with whom we have come into contact during our lives in either a fleeting or an enduring way. Living our lives when all around us characters and presences are fading away means that we are constantly redefining an order that the chaos of death disrupts at every stage of the game. Living, in some ways, is about knowing how to survive and how to piece life together again.

I have always admired man's capacity for enduring. In the twentieth century, of which I am a product, civilisations have applied their knowledge to two important and contradictory paths: the search for ever more effective instruments of extermination, and the improvement of living conditions and the preservation of the human species. In both cases they have had recourse to science: physics and chemistry for the lethal products, medicine and pharmaceutics in order to keep humans alive for as long as possible and in the best possible condition. At the intersection of these two routes some signposts appear that may briefly be summarised under the term "ideologies". Intending to indicate a direction, a use for the world and a social plan, most of the time they have filled the role of those wreckers who used to light their lanterns which they tied to the horns of a pair of oxen on dangerous coastlines so as to attract ships and cause them to be smashed to pieces on the rocks and then looted. In this case, the ships, as we know, had hundreds and thousands of men on board. Whenever I hear Monsieur Bellagar stumbling over his out-of-tune piano above my head, I seem to be hearing the music of our age in which the sickly-sweet madness of utopias that have proved to be absurd, and the bitter grief that resulted from their collapse, are mingled together.

When Eugène had completed his first chemotherapy, the check-ups showed that the tumour had been completely destroyed. My friend was cock-a-hoop. It had been a very minor business, after all. Not too bad really. Not even frightening. And as if to show off a little more, he commissioned a sort of *vanitas* by the Flemish artist Wim Delvoye, upon which he would be able to meditate at his leisure: on a wall of his study, three framed X-rays displayed the patch on his lung, a small dull black nugget, harmless and now vanished. Today they hang in my bedroom above the head of the bed, where once it was the custom to hang a crucifix.

He and I had long discussions about the malfunctions of the body, about illness and the way it is dealt with, in societies and in our organisations, about the right to take action to curb the mechanisms of degeneration or about the fact that, conceivably, since our birth, and since the dawn of civilisations, a process begins which is comparable to the countdown of a number of interior bombs whose form and activation, strengths and effects, vary according to individuals and people, and which they are unable, whatever they do, to prevent happening.

An outstanding bottle of Cos d'Estournel 1995 helped us clarify our ideas and develop them further: basically, all this was not dissimilar from the arguments that had troubled theologians and philosophers in the seventeenth century concerning the salvation of the soul, predestination, necessary grace and efficacious grace. Could what was said about the soul perhaps be applied to the body? What was the point of making efforts to maintain and look after it if in the end it was all to no avail, according to the theory which asserts that we are born in a body that already contains the seeds of its destruction and death, and that nothing – neither diet, sport nor taking special precautions – will be able to save us?

Eugène spoke of his destroyed tumour as if it were an intelligent entity. He would have liked to have known this illness within him. He was convinced that it was a sort of cyst that had accumulated all the negative charges his life had produced or undergone – unpleasant experiences, disappointments, unhappy love affairs, professional setbacks, low self-esteem.

When, more reasonably, I mentioned the Craven As and their smoke that had filled his lungs since he was eighteen, he dismissed the argument with a sweep of his hand, even though he had stopped smoking, thereby contradicting his analysis. Yet I admit that his theory, which he spelled out with obvious enjoyment and the patter of a smooth talker, interested me to the point at which, in a still vague sort of way, it produced the embryonic threads of what might be a future film.

So when do we fall seriously ill? When everything is going well or when everything is going badly? In the monotony of days that are all alike? Or else in disorder, in the breakdown of daily life? Does the sudden development of an illness such as cancer, stroke or heart attack occur because of circumstances not experienced hitherto, that upset one's equilibrium? Because of an unexpressed desire to see something happen? Because of a sense of being ground down that comes from the endless repetition of the same existence? Because of a rut that would lower all one's resistance? And can humans and illness be linked? Are we always simply victims of ourselves, or are we responsible for our own downfall?

These questions concerned me for weeks. I met a dozen doctors and researchers, some of whom doubtless took me for a lunatic, but much is forgiven artists – their side-stepping, their obsessions, their incongruousness, their tactlessness, their style of dressing – because in the end they are never really taken seriously.

The majority of these scientists recited obvious facts to me, reminding me of the causes that everyone knows – excess weight, lack of exercise, smoking, alcohol – that increase the risks of developing a disease. Two of them mentioned the onset of retirement, a sudden slowdown in activity, bereavement, divorce, prolonged

33

stress, the death of someone close, as being events that could trigger it. One of them nodded as he listened to me, his hands pressed together, and prescribed vitamins and some rest. None of them really tried to understand what I was trying to say, or rather the path along which I should have liked to lead them, although it is true that I am always a little unclear when I express myself. Words don't come as easily to me in conversation as they did when I was a teenager. It is not for nothing that I prefer images, which have the advantage of being vague and dreamlike, and which can give the person who creates them, as well as the person who views them, the possibility of experiencing them as they please.

VI

THESE BY-AND-LARGE UNPRODUCTIVE DAYS DID, nevertheless, enable me to make an unusual encounter, one with a young woman who had shared my life, without realising it, for almost a year. She was one of my neighbours. She lived on the sixth floor, in the other wing of the building. The courtyard created a space and distance of some twenty metres between us, but the fact that I lived on a higher floor to her gave me a view down into the interior of her apartment. A permanently jammed blind revealed her bedroom. As for the one in her adjoining kitchen, it was never lowered. These were the only two rooms I could see. The bathroom must have been on the other side. She had never appeared to be concerned by my presence, nor by that of other inhabitants of the building who, like me, were able to watch her every move. She left the lights on in her bedroom and in her kitchen. She was unable to live, or even sleep, it appeared, in the dark.

From the window of my study I could see seven apartments including hers. From a distance, they looked like a collection of boxes, stuck side by side and one on top of the other like a scale model, with cut-out parts of a dolls' house in which people engaged in repetitive and rarely hurried activities. I had set up my work table – a present from Eugène, "a tailor's table, nothing better for a film director: you're doing the same job, but without realising it" – in front of the window, where as I wrote or sketched, I could watch the spectacle of these lives that reflected the triviality and monotony of my own existence.

Over and above the pleasure of a voyeur, this "Rear Window" fascinated me because of the miniaturised existences it revealed. Human beings suddenly took on the aspect of laboratory mice. The water bottles, the wheels and the litter were replaced by lavatories, basins, fridges, television sets, computers, beds and sofas, but basically the difference was very slight: working people manifested a number of extremely limited activities – feeding themselves, entertaining themselves, sleeping – which was enough to define them and link them to the vast constituent body that is grouped together under the name of animal kingdom.

I had eventually come to incorporate these lives into mine, to fuse their timetables with my own, and in some ways to piece together a sort of family, none of whose members knew one another, but who, without being completely aware of the fact, shared moments in common. Occasionally, I felt the need to imagine their lives outside these boxes in which their privacy was laid bare. I lacked the social and external aspects of their existences. In this way I had come to imagine that the young woman on the sixth floor – the most recent arrival in this vertical mosaic – who I reckoned was not more than twenty-eight years old, had a pointless job, an assistant in a clothes shop, a beautician, a copywriter in an advertising agency, a sales person.

Tall, dark, with long hair that she washed three times a week, she threw off her clothes onto the floor the moment she entered the apartment at about eight o'clock every evening. She slipped on short pyjama bottoms and a very low-cut vest which she would sleep in later on. She ate a frugal supper, a yoghourt, some fruit, and occasionally a salad. In the morning, on the other hand, she had a hearty breakfast, tea, eggs, cereal, orange juice, toast and cheese. She never came home for lunch. After supper, she would lie down on her bed, on top of her duvet, place her laptop on her knees and spend hours watching the screen that lit up her face with a milky-white light, a face which, due to the distance, I could only glimpse dimly.

On Thursday evenings, she used to go out at about ten o'clock, having spent a long time trying on different outfits, all of them smart and elegant, so far as I could judge. Her bedroom would suddenly be transformed into the fitting room of a large store. Dresses, skirts, bras, trousers and blouses were despatched from her body to the floor, from the bed to her body, from her wardrobe onto her chair, and were sometimes tried on again before being discarded once more.

The fact that throughout these trying-on sessions she walked about half-naked – without a bra, wearing scanty black knickers in the shape of a horizontal band of lace across her hips that concealed her pubis behind a sparkling triangle and disappeared in a thin thread into the upper part of her buttocks, like a trickle of dried ink – had nothing at all to do with the pleasure I took in watching her.

"You're not going to expect me to believe that . . ." Eugène had said. And Florence, with whom I have dinner once a month and continue to make love with the same frequency, before these dinners, had with a glance expressed the same opinion as my friend.

And yet, whether they believed me or not, both of them were mistaken. The virtual nudity of my neighbour, even though it was agreeable to watch, played only a very small part in my enjoyment. What fascinated me about her was her indecisive nature. She seemed to me to be someone who had not yet chosen a role for herself, or rather, for whom none had been chosen: should she be a part of life, or did she belong in the structure of a novel, a film, a play, a short story? This was probably due to the fact that her existence, even more than that of the other men and women whom I saw living a few dozen metres away from me, on the other side of the gap, was invariably consistent, which I interpreted as being due to an expectation, to an indecisiveness about whether to be someone hypothetical or a real person.

The Thursday evening during which my neighbour was searching for an outfit to wear, constantly hesitating as though unable to decide on her own which role to adopt, seemed to me like confirmation that fate had set before me something that I had never until now had the opportunity of observing: a character. A character that was still hazy, ill-defined and unstable, and evolving in the mind of a creator. The real question that I asked myself was this: should I just allow things to happen, and use my young neighbour as a future part in one of my films, letting my imagination mould her and fill her out, flesh out her simple appearance, strengthen what for the time being was her relatively shallow and neutral personality with dramatic complexity, or, on the other hand, should I introduce her gradually to life itself, real life, my own, that of those close to me, by way of a meeting that I could arrange on the ground floor of the building, for example, or in the dustbin area, or else at a tenants' meeting?

My medical enquiries put a sudden halt to this dithering that I had allowed to continue, with a certain pleasure, for months when, waiting to be seen by a doctor to whom Eugène, through his daughter Ninon, who had been a fellow student, had procured me an introduction, I was sitting waiting in the corridor of the research unit of the C.N.R.S., which is situated in the southern suburbs. I noticed a young woman coming out of the office whom I did not recognise immediately, but whose features, and especially her loose and supple movements, gave me a sense of déjà-vu. I did not have time to clarify my impression since, as I was the only person to be waiting there, she looked at me without hesitation and, greeting me by name, asked me to come in.

"Forgive me for receiving you in such a cramped space. It will give you an idea, unfortunately, of the way our country treats research and researchers nowadays."

She pointed to a chair on which I sat with difficulty, for it was true that the room was no bigger than a broom cupboard. The walls vanished completely beneath shelves crammed with files and books, and there was no window to ventilate these stacks. I felt as though I had suddenly been placed between the pages of a vast tome, as though someone had wanted to imprison me in a cell made of paper, sentences, words and ink. I struggled to find a position – crossing my legs, uncrossing them – that would not get in the way of the person I had come to see. We were on either side of her work table, as small as a school desk, and our faces were so close that I was able to make out reddish flecks in her deep brown eyes that dispersed like the bits of coloured reflection that we gaze at as children in the endless mirrors of a kaleidoscope.

I could smell her perfume too, the scent of her skin, the fragrance of her breath. She had probably just eaten an orange. I was reminded of Italy, of an old orange tree laden with fruit, that I had photographed a few years ago not far from Ravello on the Amalfi coast. Its roots grew from the side of the road, on a steep slope, and the cobalt sea two hundred metres below seemed to want to entice it down from its dizzying height.

VII

"I'M LISTENING."

The young woman was smiling at me. She was wearing a white laboratory coat and holding a long pencil between her left thumb and forefinger, which she twisted to and fro, making it look as though it was as soft as a piece of marshmallow.

I tried to put some order into my muddled quest and summarised for her my enquiries and the disappointing, routine answers that I had received up till now from her colleagues, who probably approached the problem in too rational a way.

"What interests me," I said to her, "are not the physical symptoms that bring about the appearance and development of a serious illness, but the circumstances in which it occurs and why this should happen. My questions are not so much medical as philosophical." I tried to adopt an ironic smile when I used that word, so as not to lend it too much solemnity.

"I have always been inclined to think it strange that we should consider the body separately from the person who inhabits it, and that medicine should by and large treat the body as a machine, shifting the responsibility to other sciences, that are in any case looked upon slightly suspiciously, when it's a matter of understanding the difficulties and anxieties of the mind, or the impact of the environment in which the individual grows up, lives and evolves.

"The concept of somatisation is a simplistic and practical tool, but it only highlights approximately the mechanisms that I sense and which seem to me to be far more complex. But if I were to express what concerns me in another way, I would say that I am trying to think about the role that death plays in our lives, how we assimilate it into our daily routines, our activities, our love affairs, our professions, and how we strive for or against it.

"In this context, I wonder whether when illness affects us it should be viewed as a door that, intentionally or not, we ourselves open. In other words, is it conceivable that we become ill whenever we allow death to play an ever greater role, when we invite it to intrude on us in some way and to take a hold of us, whereas previously we did everything possible to confine it to an area beyond what appeared to us to be the only possible sphere of our existence?

"Obviously, I'm not a scientist like you. I think as a film-maker. I don't expect any truths. What interests me ultimately is being able one day to adapt my questions, and possibly some basic responses, into images."

The young woman paused for a while. She looked at me, still fiddling with her pencil. I very much liked this scent of oranges that exuded from her lips whenever she exhaled. I associated it with a certain happiness. With the end of autumn. That late autumn in Amalfi during which nothing exceptional happened to me, but when everything seemed to have achieved a harmony in my life. A period that lasted no more than a few weeks and I sometimes wonder whether it was, or whether it had been, the high point – as far as the harmony I mentioned, that of emotions, desires, setbacks, renunciations, dreams and their fulfilment – of my existence.

"Have you ever asked yourself who your body was in your view?"

I had just noticed that she spoke with a very slight accent, softening her "r" sounds and slightly shortening her "e's", which could mean that she might come from either a Middle Eastern country or a Central European one.

"If you had to talk about your body as a person, what would you say? How would you introduce it to other people? I'm not asking you to reply to this question now, but to think about it. I don't know what stage you are at in your relationship with your body, but the fact that you talk about death as you do makes me think that you are probably beginning to mistrust it. You are entering a phase that I call the 'inimical body'.

"For years, you have lived with it, in it, in perfect osmosis, in a harmony that satisfied you: you maintained it as best you could, and in return it procured for you what you expected from it, at the moment you expected it, physical performances, love affairs, the pleasures of eating, sensations. The benign illnesses that affected it from time to time did not cause you to question the trust you placed in it. On the contrary, they worked as reverse markers, which made you appreciate still more the majority of occasions when it was your ally. Then time slowly began to erode your partner. You have gradually grown aware of its presence, I mean its imprint, its erosion, its refusal to follow you. A bitter feeling of disassociation then becomes apparent, as in a love affair which, having been idyllic, declines. Eventually, we forget the qualities of the other person and only see what is irritating us. This can, moreover, lead to a certain form of cruelty. The unhappy partner blames his or her spouse, harasses them, causes them suffering, and even goes so far as to mistreat them. How common is this attitude, too, among those who feel that they have been let down by their body, and who then inflict on it whatever accentuates the poor and pathogenic image they have of it still further?"

I listened to the young woman. Her words resonated deep within me. It seemed to me that she was expressing very clearly some essential and obvious facts that I had never heard or read about beforehand. I spent almost two hours in the tiny office with its smell of books and oranges listening to her explain her research work to me, work that made her suspect in the eyes of the general orthodoxy because, having studied medicine and trained in psychiatry, she had changed her career path in favour of behavioural anthropology as well as psychopathology. Her work stemmed from the convergence of these different spheres of knowledge.

"Our early years are spent discovering a partner who is imposed on us, whom we learn to control, and whose development simultaneously fascinates and frightens us. The child begins to stand on its own two legs, to grab hold of things, and to guide its movements more and more subtly. The body is, as it were, a rough-and-ready instrument that transforms itself from month to month, and the child learns to explore its possibilities. Very soon it becomes a 'companion body' that fully assesses its role and justification in activities that are mostly to do with game playing. I'm not talking about the look of the body, of its aesthetic appearance, which can reveal itself according to the individual, but, rather, a little later, during adolescence, when it can act as a brake or, on the contrary, as a motor, in the relationship that the thinking being establishes with its outward appearance. In any event, the moment the stages of growth have stopped, the body is forgotten: it is there, in perfect operative mode, obeying the person who occupies it and never opposing her or him. I leave to one side the serious symptoms that may affect it; this is not the purpose of my research. It is clear that what I am describing does not apply to the physical body as an obstacle in any obvious way. Obesity, anorexia, handicaps and the early onset of cancer immediately show it to be hostile, anticipating by several decades the relationship that each individual will, sooner or later, have with it. Fortunately, these cases are in the minority among most people, and I'm interested in the norm. Let's say that from the time the person reaches adulthood, and for about twenty or so years afterwards, he or she lives with and inside a 'friendly body'. I described this relationship to you a few moments ago. The man forgets about his body because it never bothers him. On the contrary,

45

it allows him to expand his potential, and the perfect control that experience and self-knowledge enable him to acquire. It is a staunch ally, and the stability of this relationship gives the illusion that it could last for ever.

"Yet time is there, lurking in many places, in the peach blossom that withers as much as in the skin that wrinkles, the joints that seize up, the hair that turns white. But the metamorphosis that applies to the peach blossom, helping it to become a mature fruit in a few months, does not affect our bodies and so does not provide any promise. Every alteration it assumes, beyond a certain age, leads to a loss of performance and a deterioration that nothing can reverse. That is why the first signs that suddenly indicate our body is entering this process are felt by many people to be signs of betrayal. However much we may have looked after it, provided it with the best living conditions through careful diet, sport and a healthy lifestyle, it exhibits only limited gratitude because, whatever one may have done, it now operates against the person, taking no account of his or her wishes or their aspirations. Its lack of gratitude affects us.

"A 'hostile body', then 'unfriendly', 'painful', 'belligerent', and finally 'ruined': the stages follow on, inexorably, until death. They all demonstrate the supremacy that the body, the failing body, has over the mind. We can always reassure ourselves, as many a civilisation has done, by proclaiming the elderly male as the wisest individual in a society, but the fact remains that his supposed wisdom comes up against the limitations of a dysfunctional body, giving him more anxiety than pleasure, more bitterness than enjoyment. Man is only at peace with himself for about twenty – nowadays let us say thirty – years. Before, and especially afterwards, he struggles.

"Nowadays, we have set up procedures designed to cheat that attempt to mislead others and ourselves. Surgery and cosmetics do what they can to restore a happy relationship between the body and the person even when the former has already reached the stages of hostility, not to say enmity and suffering, which I have described. It's a matter of creating an illusion for the mind by means of external delusions. But its function is inevitably restricted because it does not take into account the inner perception of the body which, for its part, follows the cruel phases of the biological clock. Let's say that these days we do our very best to look good when we die. That doesn't prevent us from dying in pain and bitterness. Does it make us less unhappy human beings? I'm not sure about that. It's probably even the reverse that occurs. By disrupting the stages of the natural relationship we ought to have with our body, we increase our resentment towards it as well as our own suffering."

She stopped fiddling with her pencil, slipped it between her lips and with both hands took hold of her long hair, which she bunched together by rolling it up into a sort of spiral that she placed on top of her head, and into which she stuck the pencil, suddenly making herself look like a barbarian goddess. Her body language certainly opened my eyes. As soon as my neighbour from the sixth floor stretched out on her bed, she would rearrange her hair in that same quick and fluid way in which you can still recognise the child in the adult, its innocence, and its indifference to what others might think of it.

VIII

"AND YOU SAID NOTHING TO HER?"

Florence had drawn close to me and had laid her head on my shoulder. I was smoking one of Eugène's cigarettes. It felt good. The sun shone through the window onto our bellies. We were naked. The crumpled sheets hung over the foot of the bed, like a frozen waterfall. We had made love, like the elderly couple we no longer quite were, and it had been nice, of course.

I didn't answer Florence straight away. I had just told her about my interview with the doctor whose name was Elena, what she had told me about her research, and the sudden revelation I had had when she rearranged her hair, on discovering my neighbour beneath the features of this young research worker.

"I think that what bothered me most was the notion of distance. I felt as though it was a test. For months, someone, let's call him 'the games master', places before me at a distance a body, a straightforward-enough body, void of any real personality, that I only recognise through the movements it makes, the outline of its shape, and its relative size. I am forbidden to go near it even though

49

its nakedness is revealed to me. I am simply allowed to look at it, yet at the same time leave a gulf between it and me that I might describe as a 'crawl space', as they say in the construction industry when it's a matter of leaving a gap between the floor and the ground in a building they wish to protect from damp.

"And then all at once, at the sudden whim of whoever is holding the strings, the rules of the game are changed and I am shut away in an absurdly small room where I find myself pressed up against this very same body, but which is so close that I am unable to recognise it. Too close. I am aware of some very intimate aspects, the orange scent of her breath, the smell of detergent on her lab coat, that of a deodorant possibly, and also a slight, pleasant whiff of sweat. But focusing is impossible. Once again, I lack distance. This time I am far too close. It is never the right distance. These occurrences are a parable about the ideal distance that allows us to know people and to live in their company: neither too close nor too far. I still have to find that distance."

"With her?"

"With her. With everyone. With ourselves too. I think that's what is bothering me. I've always had a tendency to listen to myself too much. Perhaps I need to keep my distance from myself."

Florence and I had divorced in the same way that we got married. Quietly. Without any fuss. Without urgency. By mutual agreement and by mutual consent. The judge was even astonished to see that we were so complicit and so close during the proceedings. The lawyers seemed to be disappointed not to have managed to let us tear one another apart. Not a drop of blood. Not a spiteful word. Not one libellous letter.

It was also a matter of distance that got the better of us. I was constantly away. My presence was temporary, intermittent and unpredictable. Florence had wanted a husband. What she got was a blast of air. Pleasant, she used to say. Refreshing at times. Always insufficient. The times when I was writing and needed to be alone, the preparations when I was with an assistant, searching for locations with some of my team, the filming, the editing, the post-production. The life of a film-maker. A life far from her.

"Basically, it's Eugène you married, not me."

Florence was not wrong. I spent more time with Eugène than with her. We were the real couple. In life, and in death.

And then, there had been the child.

"Agathe would have been twenty-two yesterday. Had you thought of that?"

The sun had shifted from our bellies. It shone lazily on Florence's right forearm. The summer shimmered outside. You could sense the city and its drowsy noises.

"Did you hear what I just said?"

Of course I had heard.

Florence and I had almost been parents. We had almost had a child. We had a dead child. A stillborn child. Stillborn: it's one of the bluntest expressions in the language. Conclusive. There again, it is a matter of distance. A minute distance, the smallness of which confirms its absence, since the two extremes, birth and death, are blurred. Born dead. The most appalling of oxymorons. And we had given the child a name because the law does not allow one to bury anyone who has no name. Agathe. A gentle name. In appearance. A name from another age. A lost century. A child that did not appear. A name that was never addressed to a living child, but which was placed over the tiny, wrinkled and pale little body, a name like a shroud.

When I am asked whether I have children, I answer no, and I am telling the truth. But if anyone puts the question to Florence, she will reply that yes, she had a daughter, Agathe, but that she died. That she would have been twenty-two now. That she would be a young woman. And Florence would also be telling the truth, for, unlike me, Florence had had Agathe growing inside her.

Like the Toraja tree, she continued over the years to have her child grow within her innermost being. Her woman's body was filled with the presence of the little dead corpse which she never really buried but which she welcomed into her home, into her inner dwelling and into her life, moulding her according to her different ages, having her blossom into a giggling little child, then into an eternal and idealised young girl, and who took up so much room that Florence never, either with me or with Luc, her new husband, tried to have another child afterwards. Not so much from fear, I believe, of seeing a dead creature being extracted from her womb once again, as from letting someone whom life had not deigned to allow to live, but who she has taken it upon herself to make exist, disappear for ever.

I kissed Florence and went to take a shower. We always meet in the same hotel, situated in a quiet street near the Sorbonne. The staff know us. We are the couple in room 107. I almost made a film with this title. "The Couple in Room 107". I had even asked Eugène to file an application. He did so. Eugène did everything I asked of him. He never made difficulties. It's the foremost virtue for a producer: to accommodate the lunatic with whom he has decided to work. I got in touch with two or three actresses. I had a long conversation with Isabelle Adjani in a secluded tea-room on boulevard Raspail during which she made only one remark: "How very strange . . ." I had a few beers with Alain Bashung to whom I wanted to offer the male lead. We had both been reminded of Mankiewicz's fine film, "The Ghost and Mrs Muir". We talked about it for hours. The waiters in the bar eventually ushered us towards the door. Bashung died a little while later. I wrote a synopsis and made some sketches. And then I abandoned it. It was really no more than a title. "The Couple in Room 107" was not a couple. It was not a film. It was not a story that would be brought to life and would live on. Fiction is sometimes more demanding than life.

I knew that however much I washed my face I would still have the scent of Florence's sex on my skin and on my lips until the evening. I liked that. Of all the body's aromas, that of the female sexual organ is one of the most stimulating. It leaves a long-lasting mark, like a seal of appropriation, on the man who has kissed it for any length of time. We think we have captured it, but really it has captured us and obsesses us. Ghostly scents, ghostly bodies, ghostly voices. A bouquet of mingled absences and presences hovers over our lives.

I went to pick up Eugène that evening. I asked the taxi to wait outside the hospital. A month ago, Eugène's cancer had returned from holiday. It had set down its baggage in some part of my friend's brain. It no longer appeared to be interested in the lung. It was now attacking the bones. I imagined it looking like one of those stubborn and persistent wood-eating insects that gnaw at the beams of houses, hoping to make them collapse.

Eugène had told me the news as though he had announced he was going to have his bedroom repainted. I had not had time to think about what facial expression I should have put on.

"Don't look like that! You're not going to get rid of me that quickly. All this is quite normal. They had warned me."

I didn't dare ask him what else "they" had warned him about that he had not discussed with me. What would be the next stop on his cancer's tourist trip? The liver, the kidneys, the metatarsus, the intestines, the cerebellum? This taste for going on holiday and nomadic wandering distinguished the disease from many other ones, less unpredictable but just as dangerous, that preferred to settle on one organ and destroy it methodically to the very end.

Eugène was joking with a nurse while he waited for me in a room adjoining the department where chemotherapy was carried out. He still looked handsome. A slight weariness perhaps, which masked his features and made them look drawn. Slightly. He smiled as he spotted me.

"Here's my artist!"

The nurse looked at me. So that's what an artist is, she must have thought, a guy of about fifty, quite tall, quite stooped, with not much hair on his head, an expression that is both lost and youthful, who looks as though he's ill but isn't, who's badly dressed, unshaven and irritable. I am often told that I look like Jean-Pierre Bacri, which doesn't displease me for I like this actor very much even though I've never thought of asking him to be in one of my films. From fear no doubt. From fear of being too close to myself.

Eugène insisted on making the introductions last. I really must get to know the nurse. Her name was Anne-Marie. She was thirty-eight. She came from the Limousin. She was married to Simon, who also came from the Limousin. Simon was responsible for computer maintenance at a branch of Crédit Agricole. They had two children aged eight and five, Jules and Sarah. They lived in a house in Gretz-Tournan, bought in instalments over twenty-five years. Anne-Marie liked gardening and cooking. Her speciality was lamb tagine. Simon played tennis. He had a ranking. Every year they went on holiday to the Île d'Oléron, and spent a week every winter in Samoëns in the Haute-Savoie. Simon and the children loved skiing, though not Anne-Marie, who was frightened of falling. She read novels and magazines at the top of the ski runs.

I listened to Eugène conveying all this information to me without understanding what his purpose was. As for the nurse, she let him talk, maintaining her smile, allowing herself to be presented as though she was about to be assessed by the jury at an agricultural fair. She was somewhat stout and blonde and she had a pink complexion. She appeared to be in shockingly good health and at the very moment when this thought occurred to me I became aware of my stupidity. What would hospitals be like if the nursing staff, in order not to upset the patients or their visitors, looked even more ill than they did?

"What came over you with the nurse?"

Our taxi was travelling along the banks of the Seine, which in the evening light had taken on the colours of old roses. A number of bare-chested young men were walking beside the river. Some girls were wearing their bras. Summer was enveloping Paris like a linen scarf around the neck. Eugène was shivering in spite of his jacket and a light overcoat.

"I'm interested in other people."

Eugène had said this in a melancholy voice that I was not accustomed to, as though the remark contained a regret, regret that he had not put this sudden interest in his peers into practice sooner. My friend was not a selfish person in any way. He was a man of his time, no more, no less. We stopped believing in the notion of collective happiness ages ago. Our individual journey is already fairly demanding. We spend our lives worrying about ourselves. A huge project.

I opened the windows of my apartment wide. It was half-past seven in the evening. Elena – she now had a name – had not yet come home. Her empty bedroom brought to mind the stage of a theatre in daytime. I poured myself a glass of Sancerre and I thought again of Anne-Marie, the nurse. What was her real job? To welcome patients, look after them and organise the chemotherapy, certainly; to ensure the smooth working of the sessions, to check the reactions of the patients, to reassure and comfort them. But all this was a facade. In actual fact she was a warden. She stood by the doorway, on the threshold of the domain of the dead, and she observed those men and women who would soon be joining them. She knew. She knew how to recognise them. I am sure that she could tell the difference between someone who drew ever closer to the door, and another who, quite the reverse, was moving further away from session to session. Her smiling eyes contained the faces of those whom she had seen gradually fading away. Her own body retained the memory of those bodies in pain, those that she had touched, raised up, put on a drip, massaged, held tightly, washed, whose wounds she had dressed.

The Sauvignon made me think of meadows in bloom, buttercups, crocuses, asphodels, of perpetual springtime. Eyes closed, I drank in a season of freshness and rising sap. I tell myself that it really is an indifferent world that allows us to depart without restraining us. With the second glass, Florence's body returned, as did her slow smile, after orgasm, always the same, that of a cat stretching. With the third, my regrets vanished. With the fourth glass I found material to feed my sadness.

At eight o'clock in the evening, Elena opened the door of her apartment. The show could begin.

IX

IT IS TO SERGIO LEONE THAT I OWE MY DESIRE FOR having wanted to make films. I was ten years old. Every Sunday I used to go and watch a film at the Georges, one of two cinemas in the small town where I lived as a child. For the most part, they were French comedies, crude and wonderful, with simple stories as absorbent as blotting paper, and I loved them. Policemen, thieves, likeable rogues, underage crooks. The programme planning included the great hits of the time. Louis de Funès. Bourvil. The Charlie Chaplins. I lapped up some unbelievably third-rate films intended for military-service conscripts, in which you often came across actors such as Pierre Tornade, Jacques François, Grosso et Modo and Michel Galabru wearing military uniforms and in absurd situations.

We used to go to the cinema much as one might go for a walk, without bothering especially about the scenery we were passing through, but simply for the pleasure of stretching our limbs. To be in the cinema, in the darkness, to feel the presence of other people around you and suddenly see snatches of real life appear on the large screen, to feel you were involved with them, to experience at the same time what others are experiencing, to then leave the artificial darkness after the word "end" appeared, to return to the daylight, which puts each and every one back in their place, their importance reduced, and scatters those who a few moments earlier were laughing, suffering, trembling in unison: the cinema is an experience of happy moments of darkness. Happy because they are ones you can return from.

I think that for a long time I used to consider films as sorts of animated picture books. Their author was unknown. I don't even think that I thought of there being a person behind any of this. The films did not indicate any personal view about what I was being shown. I did not ask myself any questions as to how they were made. They did not seem to me to be the result of any work. And then all of a sudden there was Leone. The first person in the film world whose name I learned, whose name I remembered. Leone. Sergio Leone.

I remember the eyes of the hero, immense on the screen of the Georges cinema. Two enormous eyes that completely filled the canvas. And those eyes stared at us insistently. The idea took root. It was those eyes that were responsible for everything. For the first time, I realised that someone had decided to focus on a small aspect of the actor's expression, and to confront the audience with his gigantic eyes. Just as later on, in the same way, in this same film, he chose to make the hero's body smaller, to reduce it to the size of an ant, both he and his horse, and to lose them in the landscape, a tiny moving fragment of life in the red stone desert.

From that day on, I watched films and, indirectly, the world in a different way. I wanted to discover who made the feature film that had been recommended to me. In other words, I tried to get inside the kitchens in order to understand how the chef had chosen the ingredients, how he had prepared them, how he had thickened the sauces. And as far as other people were concerned, I no longer allowed myself to be engrossed or swayed by them, but I tried to take details from them, to define distinctive elements, to carve out a framework from them as though my eye had from now on become a camera. It seemed to me that in this way, through framing techniques, the choice of short-, medium- or long-focus lens, and editing processes, I managed to have a better understanding of what I had been plunged into. In the end, I had the illusion that there was a meaning to all this and that my life would become the film that I decided to make of it.

I waited for years before owning a camera – a Super-8 Kodak which the father of a friend had sold me for next to nothing – but I did make films at a very early age. Basically, I am convinced, cinema can manage without camera, film and auditorium. Making films is deciding to rearrange those elements that surround us. It is choosing to tell a story in which you take part. It is a bit like taking over the controls for a while.

I don't know why I am thinking about all this again, sitting on Eugène's grave. Perhaps the weather today makes one ask oneself serious questions. I often come to this cemetery. Mainly because it's a pleasant place, with attractive tombstones and large trees that shade them, independent cats that stroll haughtily over the gravel paths, and very few visitors. And then, of course, I come for Eugène. It's now almost two years since he was laid beneath the chunk of cement that has still not been covered with a monument. After a few months, this had bothered me. Now, I'm used to it. It is rather as though his grave were a makeshift one. As though he had been given the opportunity to try it out for a certain time and to return it if it didn't suit him. Satisfaction or your money back. Eugène appears to be happy with this slab that has split in the middle and is crumbling at the top right-hand corner. In any case, for the time being, he has not complained about anything.

I sit down on the grave of his neighbour, Georges Loerty (1876–1928). Beneath the dates of his birth and his death, it states that he was a poet. I tried to find a collection of his verse, in order to read a few passages to Eugène so that he could get to know him, but I was unable to unearth anything, either in the bookshops or on the internet. Or any information either about Georges Loerty. It is as though he had never existed. We stop living, but we also stop dying, as a matter of fact, many times over.

I never bring flowers to Eugène's grave. My friend didn't really like that. The most appropriate present and the one that would suit him best would be a bottle of Bordeaux, but I would be drinking it on my own and, in this place, that would not make a very good impression. Furthermore, a notice at the entrance to the cemetery points out that it is forbidden to eat and drink. "Out of respect". I don't see what respect has to with all this. Respect for whom? For the dead? The living? The food? The drink?

I often talk to Eugène, in a loud voice or in silence. I tell him what I am doing, which enables me to try to find out. I tell him what major world events he has missed. The films he would have liked – for example, I very much resent the fact that he died before seeing Paolo Sorrentino's "The Great Beauty" – the books that he would probably have given me – "You'll like this." I talk about trivial matters and how they have progressed, about Florence, about Elena with whom I now spend the night from time to time, although I skulk away in the mornings, ashamed as I am at being twenty-three years older than her and having a body that seizes up; I talk about my projected film *"La Fabrique intérieure"*, whose important lines I had picked out for him a few months before his death.

Basically, these one-way conversations are not very different from those that we had when he was alive. I've said already, one of us spoke, the other listened. The next time, it was the reverse. Now there is no next time, that's all.

I often mention Elena's body. Eventually, I crossed the courtyard. It was she who kissed me first. Two weeks after Eugène's burial. "You seem unhappy." I was. It was an odd sort of kiss, on the lips and with the tongue, but one that had a childlike or motherly touch, both comforting and clumsy. I had thought about kissing her myself, but I would never have dared do so. She really does taste of oranges and her slight accent comes from her childhood in Croatia. I noticed that it grows more pronounced when she is a little sad, or else very happy.

I don't know what she sees in me. When we are lying next to one another, naked or nearly so, or when I wake up and gaze at her, I see our bodies as being like two sides of the mountain of life. In their proximity there is something contra-indicated. I realise too that when we make love, I feel more sadness than pleasure; even though the pleasure exists, the sadness, which lies at the very depths of pleasure, is there, just as a shadow is concealed in a ray of sunshine. A sadness stemming from a disparity that is not simply to do with age. I know that I don't deserve her, and that she doesn't deserve me. Florence used to say that I was no gift. She was right. I am less and less of one, in fact.

Elena says that I am being ridiculous when I ask her what she can see in an old guy like me. She tells me to stop asking myself questions and to live from day to day. It's the expression of a young woman who has just reached the age of thirty. Who uses up time by throwing it out the window. Losing her time. Squandering it. Dispensing with it. Wasting it. All generous phrases for someone who has the immense good fortune to still have her whole life in front of her.

At my age, however, one no longer lives from day to day. We become miserly accountants. We keep a record of each minute, each hour, each day, each month. We count our coins. We don't want to be cheated by any dishonest supplier. I remember my father telling me that after eighty we finally begin to know the value of seconds, and that this brings with it a new type of sensual pleasure.

I did not conceal my relationship with Elena from Florence. We continue to meet for a drink now and then, to have dinner together once a month, but we no longer go to the previous hotel. "The Couple in Room 107" no longer exist. I think she is upset by this, but she doesn't say anything to me. She makes no judgement about my relationship with the young woman. She was not surprised when I mentioned it to her.

"You have always been dramatically predictable."

I have always very much liked the way Florence uses adverbs.

X

NINON, ON THE OTHER HAND, REACTED VERY BADLY when she heard that I was now Elena's *lover*. As I write this word I find the expression inappropriate, but what ought I to say? I'm not Elena's "husband". Nor her "fiancé". "Boyfriend" or "sweetheart" would be both absurd and unseemly given my age. "Partner" doesn't convey the truth of our relationship. "Friend" puts too much emphasis on the depths of a bond that has not yet been formed. Yes, "lover", for want of a better term. *Mon chéri*, Elena calls me. I think that's lovely. *Mon chéri*:

"Like a revolting cheap chocolate filled with a cherry and full of shitty industrial liqueur?" Ninon asked me to my face. "You're pathetic," she went on.

Perhaps. I held Ninon on my lap, literally, when she was a child. Ninon, Eugène's first child. The daughter of Eugène, therefore, and of Ludivine – what a name, you'd think you were in a Rohmer film – an actress born in Pittsburgh of French extraction whom Warhol had taken on at the dwindling Factory because she came from the

65

same town as he did, and because she had the same sort of hair as he did, real in her case, fake in his, but it matters little.

When he was young, Eugène made a documentary about the New York scene at the beginning of the 1980s. He had spent two months in the city, stunned by the dazzling verticality of Manhattan, gathering up stale crumbs as though they were gold coins from a Village that was already aping itself.

Eugène was intelligent enough to realise that what his cameraman was filming was a stage set for something that no longer existed, but this reconstruction which was sold to them as though it was some rancid hotdog was nevertheless equipped with sufficiently novel trivialities for it all to be assimilated into the framework of a post-modernism that was trying to establish itself.

In the forty-seven-minute film, we encounter Blondie; the New York Dolls, drunk and looking like carnival drag queens; one of the Ramones, I don't remember which one, perhaps Dee or the tall thin one whose first name I always forget, caught shooting up drugs in the toilets of the C.B.G.B.; Patti Smith with her Sioux chieftain's face; a number of unknown screaming or listless figures; Lou Reed, who refused to answer a question and swung a straight left at the camera; Mick Jagger, showing all his teeth, wearing a perm and a white silk suit; a few groupies who looked like whores, or whores who looked like groupies; and Warhol, backstage in a nightclub, with his three-piece navy blue velvet suit, white wig, dark glasses and cigarette-holder, smiling, worn out and very childish; and Ludivine, who had just sat down beside him, revealing her pale thighs which burst out from a very short leather skirt and her big reddish smile.

The film was called "No More Heroes". Its human value was non-existent. Its artistic rating close to zero. Eugène did not manage to distribute it anywhere. I don't even think that an enthusiastic hacker has since loaded it onto YouTube. Something that actually makes it all the more precious.

On the other hand, I am sure that seeing it today would upset me, as if I were being given the opportunity to contemplate for a second, a second or two, the nature of a stoppage time – both in the sporting sense of dead ball time in basketball, when the game has to be interrupted and one is able to apply the stopwatch, and in the full sense of a time that you find stretched out rigid by the side of a road like a raccoon in Pennsylvania, a time that has been killed by someone, or that has taken its own life, or been struck down in an attack, and which one can then, unable to believe one's eyes or rather the rhythmical beating of one's heart, take between one's fingers to examine at leisure without it draining away and escaping from us.

Would Ninon have liked me to be her lover, her own mon chéri, her old chocolate with an imitation heart-shaped cherry inside it? I who am the same age as her father, I who was his best friend?

I was given a slap when I put the question to her.

"I was joking."

"You're stupid."

"You're jealous."

"You're very stupid."

"You're just crude."

"Screw you."

"That's exactly what I say."

"You're completely pissed."

"Speak for yourself."

"Give me a light."

We went out for a smoke on the pavement. Only pavements are filled with smoke nowadays. The smoker has become an outdoor person, a fresh-air creature. Ninon was glaring at me. It would not last. I know her by heart. I love that expression, "by heart". To know by heart. The primary-school recitations. Political speeches. Women's reactions. Our mothers. Our wives. Our mistresses. Their bodies. I look as though I'm trying to be clever, as though I know everything. But I don't know a thing. I've never had a mistress. I had Florence. She was my wife. I was never unfaithful to her. Even with an actress. Especially not with an actress.

"I don't believe you. You really are drunk."

I could not care less whether you believe me or not, little Ninon. It's the truth. Actresses are all crazy and I was never unfaithful to Florence. I am not a man for more than one woman at a time. Unlike Eugène, who could not leave a woman without having already seduced the next one. A man for smooth transitions, your father. For clean splices. He was a gifted film editor, by the way. He had started off as an editor. Anyway, why should Elena matter to you, she is not your daughter, she is not you. We are adults. I am a bit older than her. But on the scale of the age of the universe, we are absolutely identical. Give us a break.

"I'm going inside, I'm cold."

"So am I."

"Shall we have another coffee?"

"I wanted to ask you. Eugène's grave. Why aren't you doing anything? That tombstone, which is crumbling away, it's ugly, isn't it? It's bare."

"Would you be happier with a beautiful grave? A beautiful death, a handsome corpse, a beautiful monument? Would that make it seem less bare? You wouldn't feel so cold, is that it?"

"Ninon . . ."

"What?"

"Nothing."

"Leave Papa where he is, that's to say nowhere. You, you're alive. How long have you got, a few years, with the amount you smoke and the amount you drink? Make the most of them."

"You're being horrid."

"No, I'm a doctor."

"What I mean, is that . . ."

"Don't say anything. Shut your trap. Stay among the living."

XI

WHAT DOES IT MEAN, THE LIVING?

At first glance, it's all fairly obvious. Separate the living from the dead. To be among the living. To be alive. But what does that signify, deep down, to be alive, as Ninon bid me do? When I breathe and walk, when I eat, when I dream, when I urinate, am I fully alive? When I feel Elena's soft and burning genitals encompassing mine and I see her eyes rise to the backs of her eyelids as though a long spell of dizziness were suddenly enrapturing her, am I any more alive? What is the highest degree of being alive? Could there be different states of being that would enable us to tell whether one was more alive or less?

And what does our body teach us about this? Not to bother about it, not be aware of it, not be concerned with it: is that to be alive? Or quite the contrary, am I supremely alive when my body causes me pain, when it suddenly reminds me about myself, mistreats me, avoids me, torments me, makes me realise that I am answerable to it, that my wonderful sense of awareness is bound up with it, dependent upon it, and that without it, awareness, however complex and sophisticated, is merely the slave of its crude actions and its minor ailments?

Elena's beauty disturbed me because it was not made for me. I was an intruder in her existence. A boor, who brought with him the anxieties and burdens of his age, with his lax muscles and his skin that was beginning to wrinkle like the surface of a windswept old glacier lake and to crack with little patches of redness; yes, an intruder, who totters in, self-invited, right in the middle of a feast of the flesh where all is firmness, pure texture and silky skin. A hand had entwined our two-time charts, attempting to merge them, to make them one, but they remained distinct and unfamiliar even though they clung to one another.

When, after making love, Elena laid her face in the hollow of my shoulder and closed her eyes, I could not rid myself of the thought that she was sleeping on death, that I was a recumbent effigy but she did not know this yet, that we were living through a dark fairy tale in which a young woman who has had a spell cast upon her falls in love with a skeleton whose terrifying appearance she alone fails to notice.

Of course, I did not mention any of this to her. Neither did I tell her that when I stroked her I was thinking of Florence and of all the caresses I had devoted to her body, which time had smoothed out, which time had wearied, but had done so with a cheerful weariness that made me love it all the more as the years went by. Girls' bodies make one think of perfect stones, polished, unblemished and out-rageously untouched. Women's bodies possess the patinated scent of those countless days in which moments of pleasure and expectation blend sensually together. They become the supple velvet of the years.

Which of the two, Elena or Florence, helped me be most alive? Making love with Florence made me confront myself. Making love with Elena forced me to become someone else. It was not a matter of starting afresh, with renewed vigour, which might well have proved to be a good thing, but of looking at oneself from afar, splitting oneself in two with disastrous consequences. I knew that our relationship could only increase a bitterness within me that had set in after Eugène's death, like some distant female cousin from the provinces, surly and dull, who arrives without warning and moves into our home without our saying a thing. We are not quite sure what her intention is: to keep an eye on us? To make fun of us? To make us understand something? To warn us? To assess us? I read somewhere that fifty is the old age of youthfulness, and that sixty is the youthfulness of old age. We cope as best we can with words. They are not going to make the cousin leave.

Even so, I did nothing to banish Elena from my own life, or to break free from hers. In cowardly fashion, I was counting on a journey to create a split in our relationship, for it is well known that travelling together can reveal habits and behaviour that are concealed in daily life and are suddenly, in some far-off place where one has no links, brought to light in intolerably petty ways. Venice had seemed to me to be the perfect destination in which to bury our budding relationship. Elena had never been there. As for me, I had set foot there twice: the first time with Eugène, for a Mostra at which our third film together, "*Perpendiculaire*", had been selected not for the official competition, but in a fringe section. The second time was with Florence.

With Eugène, I had not seen much of the city. We had rather looked down on the festival, making fun of the great trade show by drinking a great deal. I gave interviews beside the Grand Canal, on a terrace in the sunshine, and my head was constantly being turned by the gondolas that passed to and fro in front of me and the numerous glasses of Spritz that I drank like lemonade. I had even tried to punch an Italian critic in the face for comparing me with François Truffaut, which had deeply offended me. We were young, Eugène and I, presumptuous, foolish, happy, carefree. Life had not yet chastened us. Ultimately, I had seen nothing of the city. I had vomited three times in the plane's toilets on the flight home under the reproving eye of an Air France stewardess whose badge stated that her name was Marie-France.

With Florence, we had caught the train. We had arrived in the morning, still numbed by the swaying of the sleeping-car and the narrowness of the bunks. On leaving the station, the Grand Canal appeared before us, sparkling, unreal, lacquered with laughter and cries, shimmers and seagulls. It was at the very beginning of November. The weather was beautiful. The city had discharged its tourists. We stayed at a *pensione* on the Dorsoduro. In the mornings, we had our breakfast at the bar of a café on the Zattere, not far from Santa Maria del Rosario, and in the evenings, sitting in the corner of the same café, we ate whatever the Sardinian owner suggested, without us asking for à la carte or the menu: goat stew, spaghetti alla bottarga, risotto with pumpkin accompanied by a Bovale or a Cannonau. At lunchtime, we did as we pleased on the Campo Sant'Angelo, and spent a lot of time sitting in the sun after our meal, sipping small glasses of limoncello, smoking cigarettes, holding hands, bonded together by a slight intoxication and a sense of happiness that meant we were constantly looking and smiling at one another. When we were not eating, we made love or we wandered around aimlessly. Venice is the only city in the world where you can lose your way without getting lost. We were striding forward in our lives as much as on the paving stones. We were happy without really knowing it. I mean, without knowing it at that juncture, and at that moment.

I had set Elena on Florence's footsteps. Without telling her that I had made the same journey with Florence. In the mornings we had a ristretto and cornetto in the same bar on the Zattere where we also dined in the evenings. The name of the establishment had changed and the owner was no longer Sardinian, but came from Friuli. The food was still good. At midday, we had lunch on the Campo Sant'Angelo. We ate spaghetti alle vongole, or with lobster. We drank white wine from Sicily. And then small glasses of limoncello. I smoked cigarettes. Elena took my hand. The weather was fine, as it had been with Florence, but we were in March. And Florence was no longer my wife. As for Eugène, he had been dead for two years, to the day or almost, even though days are meaningless to the dead. Our footsteps led me down the same alleyways, across the same bridges, and took us along the same canals as on my previous trip, notably beside the Rio della Misericordia, along the Fondamenta Ormesini, where the city's over-extolled beauty can be savoured all the more, it seems to me, because from there it looks as though it has risen from a bath, natural, unaffected, stripped of a legendary aspect cluttered with dubious-looking golds and artificial sparkles.

Elena could not have suspected that I was making her follow in another woman's tracks, in the footsteps of an affair that no longer existed. I held her closely as we walked, just as I had walked the same paths holding Florence closely. In the evening we made love in the same little *pensione* just as I had made love with Florence there. I kissed Elena's long thighs, her totally smooth pubis which I had come to prefer like that, her belly which was so flat that it almost curved inwards, smooth and taut as a barber's strop, her lips and her tongue that tasted of the wines of the South, of strong fruit and dark berries.

I wavered in confusion for hours and years, wondering whether I wished to reconcile separate moments of my life, or to besmirch one with the other, to target the past with the present, or the converse, invent an intangible enclosure, a contest without spectators. I considered myself a bit of a shit. Basically, I didn't really know what I was trying to do by behaving like this. Elena suspected nothing.

"You make me happy," she said to me one evening.

"I'm constantly lying to you," I replied.

"Well, continue to do so." Then she fell asleep beside me, suddenly, like a child.

The day of our departure, we went to visit the Pinault Foundation on the Punta della Dogana. In one of the last of the upstairs galleries, Maurizio Cattelan's effigies were displayed. Nine bodies concealed from view by a sheet of white marble. Elena took almost no notice of them. She walked over to a circular window to admire the Lagoon and the Giudecca on the opposite shore. As for me, I reflected once more about slumber, about life that freezes, that comes to a halt and is suspended. Ever since mankind has existed, the number of men and women who have supplanted one another on earth is reckoned to amount to one hundred and five billion. Almost one hundred billion are already dead, of whom nothing or very little remains.

The bodies hidden from my view did not lie in the hieratic and codified position of effigies from the Middle Ages. Looking at them carefully, you could even mistake some of them for people asleep, couples making love and hiding themselves from our view, victims of accidents, of assassination, large burnt bodies gnarled by flames like vine shoots.

My gaze moved from bodies of marble to that of Elena at her window. I looked back at the effigies. I was proceeding from a state of being alive to one of not being alive. I considered that my position at that moment was right in the middle of these two poles. I should have liked to touch the bodies, or stretch out alongside them, to lift up a marble sheet and slip in beneath it. To take this imaginary and impossible step.

But then Elena turned round and smiled at me.

XII

IT IS THE BEGINNING OF MAY. A MAY OF RAIN AND gusting winds. The script for *"La Fabrique intérieure"* is progressing well. I write in the mornings. Do I need to mention that the trip to Venice did not have the expected outcome? I leave Elena shortly before she wakes up. I squeeze an orange for her, prepare the coffee, slip two slices of bread under the grill, put out the cereals, the fruit, the ham. I draw a heart on a sheet of paper, or lips, or my pathetic silhouette: my face with drooping eyes, a clumsy caricature on whose head I put three solitary hairs and draw parallel wrinkles on the brow. I exaggerate the sketch. I make myself look appallingly old. I'm harming myself. I depart in silence. I cross the frontier. I walk from one side of the building to the other. From one life to another. No customs officer inspects me. What would I have to declare if one did?

I arrive home. The first thing I do is look across at her apartment. Look at where I have come from, which is an odd thing to do. I have abandoned the novel that I was working on before I knew Elena. I have rid myself of the personality that I adopt every time I cross the courtyard and walk through her door. I have put on my real clothes once more.

She is still asleep. I can see her in her bed, one elbow tucked beneath her face, her long hair scattered over the sheet. The scent of her neck comes back to me with a sensual suddenness, the scent of the night, so close and just over there. Seeing Elena from where I am sitting at my tailor's table, I find it hard to believe that a few minutes earlier I was lying there beside her, in her warmth. In her life.

"La Fabrique intérieure" takes place in an imminent future. The advance of automation, of research into artificial intelligence linked to the development of artificial skin which, to begin with, had been developed for the treatment of severe burns, has made it possible to invent creatures that look absolutely like human beings, described as "Echoes" by the government corporation that has produced them. They are sorts of dolls, of both sexes, that anyone can acquire for a considerable though not excessive amount, the equivalent, say, of two years' average salary, and is then able to programme it, that is to say to construct its memory, stock it and design it. Their use for sexual ends, even though this may initially have been a motive for purchase for some customers, remains totally peripheral. What fascinates buyers is to be able to construct Echo as they please: to equip its memory as they choose, to invent a past for it, a childhood, a way of pronouncing the language, of moving, smiling, crying or sleeping. The programming possibilities are endless and, when the process has been completed, the combinations among the data open up a range of reactions that may often surpass what a simple human being experiences during an actual lifetime. Just like the computers that we use and which, even though they are designed by a human brain, carry out operations more quickly than human intelligence can, operations so complicated that our brains can neither generate nor solve them.

I tell Florence about my work. We are having coffee on the terrace of a brasserie on boulevard Voltaire. The air is gentle and humid. She is smoking a cigarette that I take from her from time to time to have a puff. She listens to me carefully. She is wearing tailor-made trousers. It is the first time that I have seen her like this. I imagine that if we were still together, she would never have thought of buying such an outfit.

"And all the people who choose to buy these kinds of dummies want them to be young and beautiful, I assume?"

"No, actually. Paul, my main character, shocks the management with an original request, for an old Echo into which he intends to implant the world's knowledge and its entire memory. A sort of exhaustive universal library, a personified internet with human, individualised features."

"God?"

"That could be one of its names, why not."

"And your creature, does it have a limited period of existence?"

"Not really. In any event its life expectancy has nothing in common with our own. They reckon between two and three millennia. Might as well call it eternity. The energy that drives it is renewable. Its synthetic skin has multiple miniature solar panels built into it.

The only way it can be disconnected is to keep it in the dark for several weeks. But that, in any case, does not harm the information which will have been stored in it, and which will remain there whatever happens. One merely has to re-expose it to the light and it comes alive again, if I can put it like that."

My final words cause her to smile. She remains thoughtful and turns away slightly towards the street. It has begun to rain once more. Raindrops can be seen rolling down the new leaves of the trees. It's very beautiful. Like giant tears that will fall on the world.

A silence sets in which neither she nor I attempt to fill. We know that we can remain like this without speaking to each other. I experienced this with Eugène too. And it's beginning with Elena. Silence sometimes seems to be the deep dialogue of those who understand one another. The low clouds drift by like distant bystanders, slightly out of focus, looking as though they have just been sketched, and not very real. I glance at Florence again. I should like to know what she is thinking about at this moment. I take a final puff from her cigarette. I inhale deeply. Voluptuously. She lets me do as I please, looks at me and smiles, a little sadly.

"It's the last thing we can still share."

"What?"

"That," she says. "The thing you are stubbing out so successfully, there, in the ashtray."

XIII

EUGÈNE'S BURIAL SERVICE WAS NOT LIKE A BURIAL, more of a sad celebration. His five children were there. Ninon, Marcel, Toine, Paule, Ludo. Standing in order of age, and side by side, their respective mothers behind them. The youngest was crying, not out of sadness, but because he was not allowed to run along the pathways.

It was late February, and that morning it was still below freezing. The cemetery looked as though it had been prepared by a special-effects technician. Frost on the hedges, the sparkle of pearls of ice on the lower branches of the trees: everything looked wonderful and everything seemed artificial. A cemetery out of a film or a fairy tale.

Many faces were unfamiliar to me. I have often observed this at funerals: the deceased seems to have had several separate lives, which have run their own course, without overlapping with any others. We often think that we are the only ones to mix with other people, who spend time with them, who get to know them. Their death confronts us with their multiplicity. There were several Eugènes.

So it's best not to be jealous or possessive. Absence places us on an equal footing. Equally, it deprives us.

I was a little far from what one might call the stage and I could not hear very well. I had arrived late. I had preferred to take the métro rather than a taxi, to be sure of arriving on time, but the trains were delayed. *Serious passenger-on-line incident.* Who could have chosen to commit suicide on the day of Eugène's funeral? I ran. I arrived breathless. I thought of Godard, whom Eugène had longed to produce. He had even laid siege to Godard's house at Rolle, in Switzerland, unsuccessfully. He had just been able to glimpse him behind a curtain, a fat cigar between his lips, looking like a bespectacled owl, observing the intruder. Godard had not deigned to answer the doorbell. Worse, he must have alerted the police, because Eugène had watched as two cars full of men in uniforms turned up. He had spent two or three hours being interrogated very courteously in a Geneva police station. They had eventually released him on the promise that he would no longer come and bother Monsieur Godard. The misadventure had not prevented Eugène over the years from taking me on a pilgrimage to rue Campagne-Première, where Belmondo is brought down by Daniel Boulanger's bullets. The service had begun. It took some time for my heart to calm down.

I wrote this last sentence a few minutes ago. I stopped typing on the keyboard, in order to read it several times. Words occasionally get coupled with a meaning that we do not intend to give them, but which nevertheless establishes itself as being more important than what we thought we meant them to say initially. *It took some time for my heart to calm down*. I was, of course, referring to my accelerated heartbeats after rushing from the métro exit, but it is the extent of the sadness that the words have accentuated. That is the right meaning, of course.

Ninon spoke, then Marcel, who is a little younger than her and who has never cared for me very much, I don't know why; he lives in Singapore where he works for an oil company whose profits he does his best to increase. Toine read a poem he had written, and Paule, at the top of her twelve-year-old voice, sang Eugène's favourite song, "*Mon enfance*" by Barbara, accompanying herself on the guitar. Ludo was crying. Not because of the song. For the reasons I've mentioned. But perhaps because of the song too; after all, how should I know? I don't know what it means to be seven years old and to be burying one's father. When Paule had finished singing, we all applauded.

And then all of a sudden, as the applause was coming to an end, the strains of another guitar could be heard in the chill air. I recognised a tune that Eugène had often made me listen to a few years ago, and then, from out of the regained silence, there was the voice, a voice that was recognisable above all the others, which began to sing the words:

> *God knows how I adore life*
> *When the wind turns*
> *On the shore lies another day*
> *I cannot ask for more.*

In the distance, standing beside Eugène's coffin, I managed to make out the lanky, elegant figure – slightly stooped as though she was holding back a perpetual sob – of Beth Gibbons, who sang, her face hidden by her fine blonde hair, and immediately beside her, the guitarist who accompanied her.

> *When the time bell blows my heart*
> *And I have scored a better day*
> *Well nobody made this war of mine*
> *And the moments that I enjoy*
> *A place of love and mystery*
> *I'll be there anytime.*

In the mid-1990s, Eugène had produced a documentary film about the group Portishead, whose lead singer was Beth Gibbons. I knew they had stayed in touch, that they dined together whenever she was in Paris, and that he visited her sometimes at her home, in Bristol, I believe.

> *Mysteries of love*
> *Where war is no more*
> *I'll be there anytime.*

He spoke to me about her from time to time ("you'd like her a lot, I'm sure") and about the subtly light, quizzical and acrobatic way, he used to say, with which she approaches life and the world. Her fragile voice, which was even more fragile that day, due to her grief perhaps, but also because of the cold that rose softly through the branches of the bare trees.

> When the time bell blows my heart
> And I have scored a better day
> Well nobody made this war of mine

We listened, every one of us, stock-still, touched by the English-woman's song which bound us even more closely to Eugène, while the notes of the guitar spun a gentle, sad ribbon around us.

> And the moments that I enjoy,
> A place of love and mystery
> I'll be there anytime.

There were actresses, actors, producers there. Many women, any number of women, beautiful, young or not so young, their cheeks rosy and their eyes misty from the cold. Some of them seemed to be transfixed in a sort of fond stupor.

> Mysteries of love
> Where war is no more
> I'll be there anytime.

Right up to the end, Eugène aimed to seduce. Right up until the final weeks, when he could no longer leave the bed in the palliative care unit where he had been admitted. "The antechamber", as he used to call it.

I spent several hours with him each day. The last conquest he had tried to make was Marguerite, one of the day-team nurses. A girl from Martinique whom I never saw without a smile on her face.

"Will you marry me, Marguerite?" Eugène asked her in my presence. "I'm as free as the air."

Marguerite laughed. She stroked his cheeks. She massaged his legs and his feet. His back. With an ointment that smelled of almonds and olive oil.

"I'm being serious, Marguerite. I'm serious, am I not? Tell her, you who know me so well!" Eugène called on me as his witness. I acquiesced. I knew he was serious. That he would have married Marguerite if she had said yes. Eugène died from being alone.

His small cancerous growth that had become larger had appeared at a period when Eugène, for the first time in his adult life, was alone. A time when he was not in love, when he was no longer with his previous partner and not yet with the next one. The cancer had slipped into the crack that love had left open. Once there, it had no desire to leave and it had methodically torn through the flimsy gap. Eugène died from no longer loving and from not being loved. It was only later that I thought of this. It is as good an explanation as any. Elena did not make fun of me when I spoke to her about it.

When he could still do so, we would both go out into the

courtyard of the hospital. Eugène in a wheelchair, which I pushed gently, for I was always frightened that he might topple forward. I wrapped him up in a couple of blankets. His head barely emerged.

"You look like E.T.," I told him.

"Don't worry, I'm not planning to fly away," he replied. It was cold. And dry.

One February afternoon, we even left the hospital grounds. On the quiet.

"Take me outside, I mean into the street. Take me to a café. I want to see a café again."

And since I made a fuss, telling him that it was madness, Eugène added:

"Consider it as one of my final wishes. Think yourself lucky to be able to fulfil one of them while I'm still alive. Not everybody gets to do that."

Fifty metres away from the entrance hall, there was a bar-cum-tobacconist shop run by a Chinese couple. Neither the barman nor the waitress – his wife? his sister? – was surprised by our curious retinue. I pushed the tables aside slightly to allow the wheelchair to pass. We settled down at the back of the room. We were the only customers. Eugène looked moon-faced, his features colourless, and dreadfully chubby and sallow. Waxy. Only his eyes had not changed. He had drawn my attention to this. The disease had invaded his entire body, but not his eyes. The eyes remain the same, from childhood to death.

We had ordered two glasses of wine – Médoc for Eugène, Riesling for me – in order to look like genuine customers, but we didn't touch them. We toasted one another all the same.

"What shall we drink to?" Eugène had asked me provocatively.

"To China," I had replied.

He smiled.

"To China!"

Eugène looked around him as though we were watching a magic show. The bar was gloomy and remarkably ugly, with a beige tiled floor, green plastic tables and chairs such as those you observe in the back yards of houses in the suburbs, alongside flimsy barbecues. The circular neon bulbs in the ceiling bathed us in an aquarium light, while on the walls there were some extraordinary stylised landscapes, made of tortoiseshell and imitation pearl, featuring rice fields and bridges over lakes. Eugène's eyes beamed with pleasure. They alighted on things, "the things of life", a life that he knew was slowly ebbing away from beneath his feet, drawn away like a worn carpet by an uncaring hand, a hand that was quite simply doing its job.

The doorbell tinkled, with a shrill, old-fashioned peal such as you still come across in films from the interwar years. A couple came in, a very tall, thin, elderly man, wearing a dark felt trilby hat which he took off immediately. He was probably over eighty. The woman, though, was somewhat younger. They made their way unerringly towards a table, like regulars, sat down without removing their overcoats and began talking animatedly, and in a low voice, in a language that seemed to me to be Central European. They looked like a couple of conspirators and, because of their age, this made them appear comical rather than worrisome.

I stopped glancing at them so I could pay attention to my friend. It was then that I noticed that Eugène appeared to be mesmerised by the man and was continuing to stare at him. I put my hand on his. He did not react. I started to stroke his hand, which was cold and swollen. Gradually, Eugène turned towards me, but at first he did not appear to see me. He then seemed to be emerging from a dream. Because I was raising my eyebrows, trying to ask him what was the matter, he whispered to me.

"Don't you recognise him?"

I glanced over again at the elderly man. I turned to Eugène and shook my head.

"Kundera. It's Milan Kundera."

XIV

I HAD READ A FEW OF KUNDERA'S NOVELS WITH A degree of pleasure, but not remembering them very clearly, I had found the film adaptation that had been made of one of his books rather weak. All I could recall of the film was the image of a buxom brunette with dark, bushy pubic hair, who danced naked, I believe, with a hat on her head. Eugène read much more widely than I did. His apartment was deceptive in this respect for the rooms were devoid of books. He did not keep any of them at home. Once they had been read, he gave them away, or left them on a bench, on a train, on a café table.

"They've got to get around, like everyone else."

Yes, now that Eugène had told me, I did recognise Kundera in this elderly man sculpted in dead wood, whose face seemed to be constantly registering a degree of annoyance or anger that he was only barely managing to control. My difficulty in recognising him initially was simply due to the fact that I had "lost sight" of him over the twenty or so years. Not that I knew him personally, but I retained an earlier image of him, from a photograph that had appeared in the press, let's say, that dated from the early eighties, or from a television appearance from the same period, I'm not really sure.

We never measure time quite so well as when we come across a man or a woman on a street corner whom we last encountered several years ago. In our memories we had retained the exact likeness of a face, the colour of hair, the skin, the appearance – all these features fixed as if in marble – and we feel assaulted by the sight of this other person, who has aged, and who obliges us to see in him or in her our own ageing process – a process that we refuse to accept and which we never really take into account so accustomed are we to our own selves and to the daily and therefore infinitesimal encroachments of time on our bodies – thus enabling us to grow accustomed to the fact gently, slowly (like the obsessive self-portraits that the artist Roman Opalka worked on daily over decades) without it producing an emotional shock. And when we look at old photographs of ourselves, it's not the same thing as meeting this acquaintance, "lost sight" of, and rediscovered, imposed, set before us without our asking, like a bill from years ago that we had neglected to settle and for which we were being asked to pay cash, right away, along with substantial interest.

The barman had just served Kundera with a coffee and a tea for the woman accompanying him – lean like him, wearing a heavy overcoat, her hair cut short and hidden beneath a plum-coloured woollen beret. They had not needed to order. They were regulars, who did not address a word or a glance at the barman when he placed the cups in front of them, so involved were they in their own conversation, a conversation in which the words were shared equally between them, each one launching into a fairly lengthy response, then allowing the other to take over and to continue for an equivalent amount of time. All this reminded me of the endless, rather boring rallies in a tennis match during the late seventies, with Bjorn Borg on one side of the net and Ivan Lendl on the other.

So what could they have been talking about with such intensity, almost hatred, even though the volume of their voices was kept low? The way in which the world's different languages take control over our bodies – facial and manual expressions, modulations of the voice, the balance between shrill, middle and solemn registers, nasal effects, guttural or reedy sounds, stresses, rhythmical breathing – can lead to basic errors in our interpretation of the speaker's intentions. I remember a scene in a small Vietnamese fishing village on Ha Long Bay where in 2009 I had gone to film images that I wanted to integrate into a video installation I had been commissioned to make by the Municipal Museum for Contemporary Art in Ghent about our notions of space, dissolution and limitation.

I had been in the Bay for three days and I had negotiated with a fisherman to go aboard his boat in which he lived with his wife and three children. I had no itinerary to give him. He should do whatever he pleased. I spent hours playing with his children. Sometimes, I helped the fisherman pull up a net. I would go up onto the bridge and lie down there. I would close my eyes for a long time, open them suddenly, and in front of me the earth was once more attempting to impose on the sea the scarred presence of tall teeth, enormous stumps driven into the green waters, buzzing with a mossy vegetation filled with birds and with noises. I slept in a hammock, which swayed with the swell of the sea and made me think that I had been provided with a comfortable place within the pendulum of a large clock of which I had been appointed keeper, in the same way as one can be the keeper of a lighthouse. Sitting in a circle, under a canvas awning, we would eat white rice, fish and vegetables. The sun seemed to me to be confused by the changing course of the boat. Sometimes, I filmed its glow on the surface of the water or the massive shadows that it tried to impose on the sea by tipping onto its surface an entire sweep of jungle and cliff.

In a small port where we had dropped anchor, I had gone ashore to walk around the village a little, a few straw houses at the very most, the beginnings of a road in which children played with a black pig on the bare ground, a dog and four hens. All of a sudden, an incredibly violent argument erupted a few yards away.

Five men were squatting around a plastic bowl out of which some large, pale fish that looked like sickly carp occasionally poked their mouths, white and scattered with barbells, to gasp for air as though they were begging for help. The two men who were opposite one another were yelling even louder than the three others. Their voices clashed like swords, producing sounds that were simultaneously muted, shrill and curt. Each of them waved a threatening hand at the other, which was sometimes directed at the fish or other individuals, and ended up being pointed at the person whom the speaker was addressing.

The intensity of the argument was such that all the noises of the village seemed to have been blotted out by the voices that hurtled into one another. Suddenly, the two men stood up, their faces drew ever closer to each other, and their features seemed to me to become more deformed, as in a rapid process of anamorphosis. Their colleagues stood up too, lending their gesticulating bodies to the battle, as well as their voices and their utterances, which I could hear were clearly not Vietnamese, though I was unable to understand whether they were words of appeasement or words that encouraged hatred and scuffles.

I was wondering whether to intervene in some way in order to calm them down when suddenly the shouting stopped. One of the two men, the more vindictive one, took out a bundle of banknotes from his pocket, which he counted quickly and handed to the man opposite him on the other side of the bowl. This one counted the notes again and gave a sort of nod of acquiescence. The first man leaned over the bowl, grabbed two fish by the gills, held them up in the air, examined them all over, and since he appeared to be satis fied with them, he also gave a nod and disappeared together with two of the onlookers.

What I had taken to be an altercation that was reaching a crescendo was merely Chinese men haggling. All this had taught me that our bodies, our movements, our voices can only be read correctly and without misinterpretation within a circumscribed bubble, which is the culture in which we have grown up or in which we have lived long enough to know the keys to understanding it.

Could Kundera and the woman who was with him have been talking about love perhaps, exchanging ideas and sweet words, sentences of infinite tenderness, of which I only detected the uneven surface, clumsily planed down, deceptively cold and rough?

XV

EUGÈNE COULD NOT TAKE HIS EYES OFF THE ELDERLY man. He seemed fascinated and the writer was not aware that he was being observed in this way. I pointed out to my friend that time was going by and that we should perhaps think of returning to the hospital before Marguerite sent out the security officers to search for us.

"Let me stay here a little longer," Eugène replied, without even looking at me. "I don't know whether you realise fully what this fortuitous encounter means to me. That man you see there, who appears to be nothing other than an old guy in perfect health, whereas I am merely an insignificant creature who's ill, has without a doubt been the writer who has mattered more to me than anyone else. It is to him that I owe some of the most precious and fruitful moments of my life. In reading him, I felt that I was going to the heart of the way in which the portrayal of life, and life itself, can be admirable, absurd, grotesque, boring, unique and laughable. It also seemed to me that thanks to his novels I belonged to a European continent of literature and thought, to a space that only those

97

books produced by the greatest minds can describe and where every reader is welcomed as a distinguished guest.

"I know that we really owe who we are to our parents of course, to school teachers, to professors perhaps, but I am convinced that we owe a great deal of our private and emotional make-up to artists, whether dead or living for that matter, and to the works they have produced and that live on, in spite of their ebbing away, in spite of time that erodes the smiles, the faces and the bodies. That's why I wanted to do this job. I knew I wasn't an artist. But I wanted to live as close as possible to them. To help them as best I could to accomplish their work. It's possible that I wouldn't have been here with you if I hadn't come across this man's books. My life would quite probably have been different. I don't say it would have been worse or better, but it would have been different. You and I might not have met. Can you imagine? He gave me a portion of his strength, his obstinacy, and his intelligence too. Reading him was like listening to a voice that you wanted to stifle. It was to go against a certain sense of history that imposed upon millions of men a control and an amputation of their basic liberties."

It had been weeks since I had heard Eugène talk so much, and with as much energy. Every day the disease took a toll of his energy. Occasionally, when he dozed off in his bed and I was sitting beside him, I would gaze for a long time at his face that had become almost unrecognisable, at his emaciated body; I would think of those peaceful landscapes, in the countryside or in the forest, that are suddenly handed over one day for some building or commercial project, and on which you then see plant machinery swoop down, hostile and plodding, and looking like giant insects, excavators, bulldozers, diggers, dumper trucks with outsize wheels which, having ravaged the surface beauty in a few hours, burrow methodically and persistently into the interior of the site, ripping out the vital organs and all the entrails, boring into the depths, scouring, draining, planing, only to leave, after a few weeks, nothing but a gigantic bare hole, a kind of field of operation from which all living matter will have been extracted and into which they can now pour tons and tons of dead concrete.

Bodies fade like flowers in vases; their corollas droop one day then slump in an irreversible destruction of their colours and their scents. Even the clear water from which they drew their beauty and their scent begins to be disturbingly murky, as though their death became apparent in a grimy and foul-smelling precipitate. Marguerite's smiles and jokes managed to produce no more than a grimace on Eugène's countenance, which he did his best to make look jovial, rather like a clown who one never really knows whether he is laughing or crying. He had given up his proposals of marriage, but when the nurse massaged his temples, his arms or his neck, I could still see how much the contact with this female body and the restrained but genuine affection with which she stroked my friend brought him a radiant pleasure, and at such moments I could sense him growing more relaxed, unwinding, loosening up, and, with his eyes half-closed, casting off into some memories of love and gentleness, embraces and brief moments of pleasure that the memory still managed to revive brightly just when his body was exuding nothing but rejection, inconvenience and pain.

But, to return to the scene in the bar, to the transfiguration that I witnessed, I was aware – on that cold February day, when one wondered whether the pale light was due to a partial eclipse, to a cloud of particles shedding its dull glimmer into the Parisian atmosphere, or to a celestial bereavement – how much literature can sometimes matter more than life, and also how much literature manages to make life more alive, can reawaken it and drive away – for a limited period of time, alas – whatever is gnawing at it, wearing it down and destroying it.

Eugène had closed his eyes and was reciting some of the titles of Milan Kundera's books, murmuring them as if they were a poem: "*The Joke, The Book of Laughter and Forgetting, The Unbearable Lightness of Being, Life is Elsewhere, The Farewell Party.*"

He spoke them in such a low voice that the elderly writer, still immersed in his discussion, obviously did not hear him.

"His voice did not just come from the East," my friend continued. "It had not just risen up from the other side of that wall that was later pulled down, it came from those human depths in which our marvellous and complex strivings are to be found. It wove together our woes and our splendours, our imperfections and our beauty. It made me feel more of a man and more free. It inflated my lungs. It has been my life blood. I remember that when I held one of his books in my hand for the first time, the latest to be published, I could feel myself quivering as I would prior to a vitally important meeting, and if anyone had asked me to choose between reading one of his books or spending the night with a girl, I would not have hesitated for a second. And yet, you know me . . .

"He who used so much irony in his work," Eugène went on, "would probably find this comical: the dying man who is given one final wish, to rub shoulders for a few moments, in a shoddy bar run by Chinese people, with one of the men who has mattered most in his life. Are you going to tell me that this is not a demonstration of the mischievousness of someone who takes pleasure in playing around with us like poor laboratory mice?"

"All the same, you're not going to start believing in God, are you?"

"No, that would be too simple. And then it would be too late. I leave last-minute bets to those who are dying of fright."

"Why don't you tell him all that you have just told me? Would you like me to push your wheelchair towards his table?"

Eugène raised his hand to halt any attempt to do so on my part.

"Come on now, look at me. I'm in no condition to inflict myself on others. I'm no longer viewed on equal terms. I've already been excluded from the card table. At best or at worst, I'm looked upon with pity or with distaste. I'm not seeking either of them. Kundera has written some important books, but all the same he can't cure hopeless cases. Leave me here for a few minutes longer. I find it really amusing to be breathing the same air as him. The earth is so small, and I've been so happy here."

We left the room a little while later, trying to make our exit as quietly as possible, but just as I tried to make Eugène's wheelchair swivel between two tables so as to point it in the right direction, I knocked into a chair which scraped the ground, making an unpleasant noise. Kundera immediately stopped talking and glanced over in our direction. He took absolutely no notice of me and only had eyes for Eugène at whom he looked with a neutral gaze. He reminded me in that moment of those great masters of medicine who, at the mere sight of the patient, thanks to a set of symptoms which only they are able to read and interpret, can make a diagnosis that will subsequently confirm all examinations.

Kundera's expression gradually lost its apparent coldness and his facial features, the lines of which had been shaped by his discussion into a stubborn and hostile web, relaxed. Then a smile appeared on his lips, and his eyes, beneath the double arch of his bushy eyebrows, lit up with a childlike gleam. He greeted Eugène with a nod of the head that was not merely a simple and casual expression of passing politeness, but on the contrary, as in one of his books in fact, a gesture into which, beneath the simplicity of appearances, he managed to slip unexpected depth.

On the pavement, Eugène, ecstatic and covered in blankets up to his head, looked up at the grey sky and, in a rasping and joyful voice, kept on muttering: "E.T. go home . . . E.T. go home . . .", not realising that in the distance, at the entrance to the hospital, a furious Marguerite, accompanied by two porters, was gesticulating and raising her fist at us.

XVI

EUGÈNE'S COMMENTS, AS REPORTED BY ME, ARE obviously not the exact phrases he used. However, I have no intention of putting words into his mouth. I am trying to be faithful to him, yet in spite of my efforts, memory and language create a sort of refocusing of a reality that undoubtedly existed, but which belongs to a past that is receding. I am aware that writing is an interment that shrouds everything as much as it brings things to light. Cinema does not operate in the same way, but it is true that it is not composed of the same ingredients either.

Eugène's voice, though it remains clear and alive in the part of my brain where the sounds that affect me are preserved, could never be reproduced in my sentences. The language that I bestow on him is actually mine because, apart from a few moments when, like flashes of lightning, his words break through the memory and settle into my narrative, they cannot exist without me, without my intervening. That is why, alas, contrary to what would have happened had I filmed him during our conversations and in the scenes that I describe, it is impossible for me to give either the slightest notion of the texture of his voice, its inflexions and its tempo, or of his gestures or the way his face would light up. And however much I might make it a point of principle to describe with obsessive precision the way in which his features would alter during the course of our conversations – which I remember perfectly – the effect would become artificial because I would have the impression that I was producing a succession of close-ups, macrophotographic ones, whereas each of us knows that the general and immediate impression we gain of the person who is sitting in front of us is an impression that is indeed made up of hundreds of details, but which are sensed and worked out in a fraction of a second and not recorded one after the other.

My friend is reduced to a simplified presence. His body is stripped of its numerous dimensions and, through my endeavour, becomes nothing more than a flat cover, both accurate and inaccurate, just as a folding tourist map of a town may be in comparison with the place that it features, or a topographical map compared to the landscape that it reproduces.

Normally, I use words to express actions, to introduce settings, within the framework of a script. The language then takes on a mediocrity and accuracy worthy of an instruction manual for a household appliance. It is merely a question of giving readers an idea of what the setting in question could be eventually, on a screen. For some time I have been discovering what language can provide when its purpose is to serve nothing else but itself. I have taken on this book as though I was hoping to continue a conversation that has been interrupted, as though trying to weave a flimsy, invisible trap capable of capturing voices and lost moments.

Eugène's death did not only deprive me of my best and only friend. It also removed any possibility I had of uttering or expressing the things that troubled and frightened me. Equally, it meant that I lost the voice and the words that I enjoyed hearing and that sustained me, and which gave me, much as a radar system operates, an understanding of the world which, alone now, I only manage to cope with imperfectly.

With Eugène gone, I have realised how much our friendship was a friendship of words, and how much these words that we exchanged had, over the years, established for me a framework for that house that we all attempt to construct with patience and difficulty and which is called life. Eugène's death interrupted the building work. If certain rooms are completed and are to my satisfaction, many others need attention of one kind or another, while others are still only at draft stage on the architect's table.

Today, it seems to me that, thanks to this free-flowing narrative, its layout and its development, not only am I obliging Eugène to remain near me, I am also keeping him on a sort of life-support machine, in a coma that is not exactly death, but at the same time I am able to resume work on my house. I probably make slower progress, and I work less well than when there were two of us. But I continue. By the same token, the writing becomes the place where our friendship meets. Eugène is here, in the pages, in the lines, or between them. The narrative is his bedroom rather than his tomb.

And Ninon is right: it matters little whether the tombstone is made purely of cement and crumbles after a few months. Eugène is no longer beneath it. He is here. The text has become the Toraja tree.

Elena wants me to go to Croatia with her this autumn. She wants to introduce me to Pula, the coastal town where she spent the first ten years of her life. The slight accent she still has, like the trace of perfume on skin, is testimony to this childhood. The fact that she hasn't lost it, that there is still within her a part of the child she once was and which doesn't want to leave the dance, touches me greatly. I haven't said yes, I haven't said no. I haven't said anything. I am kicking it into touch. I am making the film project my excuse. What would the world be like if we all told the truth?

XVII

EVER SINCE I'VE TRIED TO MAKE FILMS, I'VE BEEN IN the habit of completing the scripts in the house where I spent my childhood, in the bedroom I had there, beneath the roof, and which my father, at my request, had covered in pine panelling when I was twelve years old to make it look like a room in a chalet or a mountain refuge hut. A single fanlight window lets in a sparse light above the bed. The desk is also made of wood and is attached to a corner of the wall. On summer evenings, by lifting up the fanlight and performing a slight acrobatic manoeuvre, I could hoist myself up onto the roof. I smoked my first cigarettes there, dreaming of rock climbing. I looked up at the sky. I listened to the call of the frogs that rose up from a pond at the bottom of the gardens that my parents tended. My future life seemed to me as vast as the Milky Way, each luminous dot representing a day in this life, the brightest of them signifying the most intense and unexpected of the days to come. The smells of hay and animals blown in by the wind slightly intoxicated me, unless it was the first taste of tobacco, mentholated, that I smoked there on the quiet. I was happy. I was waiting for everything to begin.

I am a bad son. My mother is not dead, and I only visit her occasionally. If I say that she is not dead, it is because I cannot bring myself to write that she is alive. She is barely so. Or differently. In a way that the majority of human beings do not recognise. Her body survives in a wheelchair, in a retirement home in the small town where we have lived. They place her in it after having washed her, got her out of bed and dressed her. She is wheeled into a communal room where she mingles with other wheelchairs occupied by women and men as silent and hunched as she is, whose sparse hair has become unmanageable, whose tearful expressions gaze endlessly at the floor and whose shrunken mouths dribble slightly, fed with clear soup and purée, flans and yoghourts, with a spoon, like very old childlike bodies.

Now and then one of them lets out a brief cry, which encourages a second from another inmate, and a third from yet another, and so on, and you suddenly have the impression of being in a zoo in a botanical garden, where in the glasshouse there live a few animals that are almost a hundred years old, belonging to a species you thought had perished, who demonstrate their forgotten existence in a brief and heart-rending manner.

On each of my visits, I am unable to spend long with my mother. When I look at her, I see the clumsy sketch a third-rate artist might have drawn of her, getting her features wrong, the proportions of her body, the outline of her figure, the shape of her face. Over time, the jaw has filled out in every direction. Enormous and bony, it predominates, consigning her eyes that were once so lively and pretty, her eyebrows, her forehead and her nose, to a background of very minor interest in which they have eventually hardened and become sunken in. Her brain, even though it no longer functions, seems to weigh a great deal and to be drawing her entire skull and body forward, as if she were about to fall. This, however, does not happen because the staff strap my mother and those like her into wheelchairs with safety belts that emphasise the meagreness of their bodies, their gradual fading away, their decline.

She who was a large, plump woman now looks like a small, crumpled thing, confused, shrivelled, wasted away and always feverish; shivering too, like the featherless fledglings that I used to discover in their nests in the spring, their flesh so transparent that I could trace their entire vascular system, and their enormous heads, punctuated with two still-blind eyes beneath eyelids knitted together, nodding gently on their scrawny necks, too weak to support their weight for long, and chirping feebly through their large, open yellow beaks when they became aware of my presence.

I sit down beside her. I take one of her hands in mine, like a branch of burning flesh, which I stroke as I talk to her, forcing myself to carry on a bogus conversation in which I can sense she is not aware of anything, telling her a little about my life, the weather, the changes I have noticed in the small town, but my voice soon seizes up and fades like the volume on a radio in which the batteries suddenly give out. In the end, I fall silent. We are silent side by side. I feel ashamed calculating the minutes that have just elapsed. I glance at my watch. The time in here is not that of the world outside. It has a viscosity which agglutinates every second, which amasses the hours in a weighty, rather unearthly cluster. I tell myself that I should stay a while longer. Out of common decency. I tell myself that she is my mother and I am her son, even though each of us now belongs to milieus that never meet. That she is part of a world I know nothing about, in which I don't know whether suffering, pain, dreams, memories and time exist, and that she no longer knows anything about my world, cannot understand in the slightest what I experience, what I feel, or what my existence is like.

Her entire life is concentrated in the rapid throbbing of blood through veins that now seem to want to break free of her body, to be rid of it, as is evident from the way they protrude from her skin, thus making the surface of her arms look wizened, as though a network of roots has suddenly appeared there, blue or violet depending on where they are, sometimes marbled with patches of dark, mauve or black, relicts of tiny haemorrhages caused by anti-coagulants. There is the breathing too, measured and of minimal range, in which each in-breath appears to require a painful effort and each exhalation seems to be the last, occurring with the raucous rhythm of a death rattle, both motions being separated by a lengthy interruption, an apnoea that seems interminable to me, but which is not yet death.

Elena came with me to the station. On the platform we acted out a scene in which people who love one another are splitting up. Elena was not acting of course. She didn't have to pretend. Nor did I have to pretend, but it always seems to me that behind my shoulder another self, disenchanted, mocking and poisoned with irony, is framing me and making fun of me. I haven't shot any of my films in a station and so I have never filmed a couple who were saying good-bye to one another, who were separating for a week or for good. Probably because this scene clutters up thousands of films and in the end says nothing new, not signifying anything other than what is shown. More likely, no doubt, because I would not know how to film it. I could only reproduce what has been done by many others before me, for I need to believe that what I am doing has never been done before, at least in the way in which I am doing it, even if that is untrue. Otherwise, how could one go on?

I found the way in which Elena gradually disappeared as the train started to move very beautiful, the way she left the frame even though she was standing still, the way in which her body seemed to be a part of the material hardness of the platform, with only her right arm raised, the way she lifted her hand to her lips and sent me a kiss that I could only half-receive because the frame eclipsed the other half, yet almost immediately, thanks to the continuous track-ing, other women appeared, and even some men who were also blowing kisses or waving their hands, dispensing irritated or joyful *au revoirs*, fragments of which I received even though they were obvi-ously not meant for me, without my ever being able to observe the faces of the men or women for whom they were intended, despite my being in the same place as they were, a disconnected place, that picked up speed, took us away, separated us mechanically from those we loved, and in which shortly, after ten or fifteen minutes, the majority of passengers would fall asleep, as though the railway company in addition to transporting human beings was also responsible for plunging them into a deep sleep.

I sleep in the bedroom I slept in as a child. I eat my meals in the kitchen I knew as a child. I reread and correct the script of "*La Fabrique intérieure*". I call on my mother in the late afternoon. I talk to Elena on the telephone in the evening, at length. It's as if I could see her, stretched out on the bed, in pyjama shorts and a vest. She is putting the last touches to her doctoral thesis which she must defend in a few months' time. We are nothing more than two disembodied voices. I wonder what the world would be like if human beings were reduced to their voices, if all our bodies suddenly vanished and there were nothing left but our voices. Would we be any better off?

At the end of our conversations, Elena tells me that she is sending me a hug and she imitates the sound of kisses which are distorted when they reach me by the poor quality of my phone, which I am reluctant to change because it still contains, like an old, worn-out brain, all Eugène's messages. I have the impression that Elena's kisses are obliged to pass through glass walls in order to reach me and that their sweetness is affected by this, or that someone is attempting to distort their delicate sound and make them grotesque and ridiculous, but is unable to do so. Her kisses find me and affect me. I ought to write instead that I am surprised to be affected by them. What most disturbs me is that I carry on these evening conversations in my bedroom, stretched out on the bed

I slept in as a child, and as I listen to Elena and talk to her, I am no longer sure what period of my life I am in, so strongly is this place linked to those far-off years, and it is not just me who receives Elena's kisses, but also the twelve-year-old boy who had never yet kissed a girl and who dreamed of doing so as some remote unattainable thing. Thus Elena, in a strange confusion of time, becomes my first lover.

Every morning, here as elsewhere, I wake up having had the same dream, and I've done this for years. I believe it began about ten years ago, for no reason: I am in an unspecified place, in bare surroundings. I hold a revolver in my hand. Very quickly, without thinking, I slip the gun into my mouth and fire. Occasionally, there are a few variations: I press the gun to one of my temples, or beneath my chin. The procedure can also be different: sometimes I hang myself, I hurl myself into empty space, I slit my throat, I throw myself under a train, or a truck driven at high speed. This dream of violent suicide is a daily occurrence. I kill myself and I wake up. I wake up after the explosion but before the bullet has shattered my skull. The day can begin at last. It's never frightening or tragic. It's not a nightmare. It's a starting point. It's life.

XVIII

WE NEEDED TO FIND A WAY OF HELPING EUGÈNE'S
production company to continue to exist. Two months after his
death, Ninon, Marcel and I received the same letter sent on to us
by a lawyer. Each was handwritten. It was the first time I had
received a letter from Eugène. He had had to die in order that he
could write to me. And even though the time that had elapsed
between the moment of his death and receipt of the letter could be
explained by the fact that the lawyer was merely respecting the will
of the deceased, I nevertheless had the weird impression that the
dead still had the ability to write letters, and that somewhere there
existed, illicitly, a postal service used solely by them.

The handwriting was jerky and clumsy. Reading the words, I
realised that whoever had written them had had some difficulty
doing so. The date at the top of the page referred to a period, mid-
October 2012, when Eugène was still trying to mislead me by treat-
ing his recurrence as a benign secondary effect. Perhaps he had
written the letter when he was in a great deal of pain, or after a

chemotherapy session, in an uncomfortable position, without support, and with his arm hampered by the drip-feed?

In his message, he urged us to come to some agreement whereby his company should not be sold at auction, for the list not to end up in the hands of just anyone, that what he had achieved should "last a while" – those were his words.

This was how Les Films d'Eugène came into being. It took more than two years nonetheless. Two and a half years to be precise. Legally, for reasons I have not attempted to understand, it was complicated keeping the old company going, but simpler to create a new one out of it in which Ninon, Marcel and the other, underage children, represented by a lawyer, an acquaintance of Eugène's whom I had not met, were to be the majority shareholders. I, for my part, owned ten per cent of the capital, which Eugène, without telling me, had bequeathed from his former company, as well as a book, which would be the last book he ever gave me, *The Sergeant in the Snow*, by Mario Rigoni Stern. On the flyleaf he had written: "You'll like this."

I read the book. I did like it, of course. And afterwards I read all the other books written by this author, who basically always tells the same story – the seasons, wars, human beings, the landscape of a poor mountainous region in the north of Italy – but he does it so well that you take a simple and profound pleasure in reading it, and especially rereading it, as though you are listening to well-known stories over and again, told by a voice that is nearby and is attractive. In *The Sergeant in the Snow*, there is a brief passage that Rigoni Stern wrote after the suicide of Primo Levi, who was his friend. In 1945, both of them had had to cross the Europe of the dead on foot in order to reach their homes. They had each published their first book in about the same year, but I don't believe either of them ever felt that he was a writer by profession. It was circumstances that had driven them to write, in order to try to tell and survive.

In his passage about Primo Levi, Rigoni Stern describes his own excursions on skis, in the silent, snowy winter. He is never alone at times like this: a friend who has died always accompanies him, with whom he makes his way, appreciating the pure air, the gleam of the sunshine in the frozen distance, and deciphering the tracks left on the ground by the wild animals. On that particular day it is Primo who slips along on skis beside him, although there is no shadow stretching out behind. Both of them rediscover that dialogue and that bond which not even death has managed to destroy. I often reread this passage. I only have to change the names to recognise ourselves, Eugène and me.

Ninon, Marcel (who could not give a damn, having always regarded cinema as an activity for children who refuse to grow up, and he is quite correct in my view) and the lawyer have entrusted me with recruiting someone capable of managing the firm. I gave the job to Kim Soo, who had been the production manager on several of my projects, who knew Eugène well and who likes the films that we enjoy. If all goes smoothly, "La Fabrique intérieure" should be the first full-length film produced by Les Films d'Eugène.

We celebrated the birth of the new company. Marcel had already left for Singapore. Aeroplanes don't wait, any more than the price of oil does. There were about ten of us, and the younger children were running around in all the rooms. Their mothers were talking among themselves, as they would at school collection time or the end of a birthday tea party. Elena had come with me. Ninon introduced me to a certain Max – "someone of my age" (she meant her own age, of course) she whispered pointedly in my ear – who never stopped sending and receiving messages on his mobile. In profile, he looked like Hugh Grant, but when one was face to face with him, his features accentuated an imbalance on the left side, as though he were made of celluloid and had been standing too close to a source of heat. I told myself that there were some people who should only be seen from behind, or from one side only, or not at all. I wondered what impression I gave other people, what image my body suggested when I was looked at from behind, or from the side. We always live with a partial image of ourselves. We never see ourselves as others see us. To ourselves, we are nothing more than a flat, frontal surface most of the time, never a moving shape, a whole body perceived in space that is sculpted within this space three-dimensionally. Only the film actor, if he sees his own films, which is not always the case, can have this complete vision of himself.

"How do I look from behind?" I asked Elena, who came by at that moment and stroked my arm as she passed.

She frowned and then laughed as she disappeared. I turned towards Eugène, a large framed photograph of whom now adorns the small entrance hall of the offices. I hadn't seen this photo taken by Studio Harcourt, in that velvety half-light that characterises the style of this firm whose fortunes have long been linked to the legends of cinema. The photograph dates from the early days of the discovery of Eugène's illness. Ninon told me this. It was she who had wanted to hang the photograph in this position, but it had been Eugène who had wished to be portrayed in this way. Eugène is looking at the visitor. As we push open the entrance door, Eugène welcomes us, his chest inclining forward slightly, a glimmer of a smile on his lips, his chin resting on the closed fist of his left hand. I recognise him, of course, but it is not entirely him, probably because he is posing, because of the studio lighting, the slight retouching applied to his features, and the size of the portrait which makes his face look four times larger than it actually was; all of these take from the impact of the picture. It is not the Eugène whom I knew. It is not the lifelike Eugène. It is an in-between person who looks like him, but whom I never met.

At home, on my tailor's table, I have a picture of him among countless other objects: photographs of my mother and my father when they were children, of myself, also as a child, snail shells, a dried pomegranate that has lost its colour and its substance, but has retained its exact shape, pots containing pens, lighters, notepads; a complete hodgepodge that is the size of a modern-art installation and which I have promised myself to make into a film, a short film that would relate the life of a person through the objects placed on their work table. The photograph of Eugène that is in front of me every day is one that appeared in *Le Monde* with his obituary, and which I cut out. I glued it onto a piece of card. Eugène is sitting at a café terrace, next to a small, round, marble-topped table. He is holding a cigarette in his right hand. He is not looking at the camera. His face and his eyes are turned to the right. He does not appear to be staring at a precise point, but out into the street. The weather is fine. He is wearing a shirt. All this is very natural. He has a melancholy smile. Or rather, I find his smile melancholy. I like the fact that he is not looking at the person looking at him. This makes the photo a little less solemn. His presence becomes less weighty, and his absence less intense. I don't think that I could work very long with Eugène gazing at me. I would constantly be wondering what he was thinking of me. He would distract me. I would talk to him.

Kim Soo tapped me on the shoulder. He was looking at me with a big smile on his face. That evening, the newly appointed manager of Les Films d'Eugène was also acting as waiter. He never stopped coming and going, filling glasses, handing round spring rolls and samosas assisted by Maguy, the old secretary; I say "old" because Eugène never stopped saying "my old secretary", even though Maguy was exactly the same age as him. He used to talk about her affectionately as though she were a piece of furniture and said that he had inherited her when he bought Z.K.Z. Movies, a firm that specialised in making X-rated films and whose best days, in the late 1970s, lay in the past.

In those days Maguy was already responsible for the secretarial staff and the accounts, but Eugène and I were surprised a few years later, when among the archives kept in a box in the cellar we came across a pile of videos still wrapped in cellophane and realised that Maguy had also taken part as an actress in some of the productions of Z.K.Z. Movies, among them *"Comtesses en rut"*, *"Lascives en laisse"*, *"Les Fleurs du mâle"*. We had never mentioned our discovery in her presence. It was her secret and it was ours.

She was now a small, plump, likeable woman, who looked five or six years older than her age, who always dressed in autumnal colours and who had recently become a grandmother for the second time. Occasionally, when I watched her, as she was chatting to me about certain accountancy details, or handing me train tickets, or checking times of meetings with me, there suddenly – and completely unintentionally as far as I was concerned – came to my mind some of the shots from the films that Eugène and I had watched, and from Maguy's actual body there emanated her former body, as if it were emerging from a muddy membrane, or from a kaolin shell taken out of the oven and which you break so as to extract a piece of pottery that you had been baking there, and which is then revealed, perfect and pure. But it was impossible for me to connect her twenty-year-old body – naked and slender, with its thick black bush, its dark armpits, her hair drawn into two plaited bunches, and which three gentlemen with moustaches and permed hair were caressing and penetrating one after the other – with her present-day plump body, constantly concealed, summer and winter, by layers of material, scarves, pullovers, long tunics, shapeless trousers, Indian blouses, and hand-knitted bonnets, from which only her face emerged, round as an apple, crowned by short pepper-and-salt hair, and accentuated by a double chin that created a sort of soft collar around her neck.

"Are you dreaming? Shall I pour you some more?"

I held out my glass to Kim Soo.

Eugène in his frame seemed to be laughing at me.

XIX

THE FOLLOWING NIGHT, I WAS UNABLE TO GET TO sleep. I had chosen to return to my own apartment and let Elena go home on her own. She had to get up early. I could sense that I would not want to do so. We had left one another in the hallway of our building after hugging and kissing in the porch like two furtive teenagers.

I was at that indeterminate stage when I considered the finished script satisfactory, but did not yet know whether the approaches we had made to the C.N.C. (*Centre nationale du cinéma*) and the television chains to raise the finance would succeed. This plunged me into successive states of excitement, impatience, despondency and edginess. I consulted my doctor much more frequently than usual, for a yes or a no. I would discover all sorts of pains, stomach aches, palpitations, insistent migraines and abnormal heartbeats. Eugène knew me backwards and at times like this he used to have a case of Bordeaux delivered to me together with the recommended dosage.

When I got home, I had found a message from Florence on the

answering machine. "Nothing special," she said, "I just wanted to know how you were." There was a hint of forced levity in her voice. I also sensed a subdued sadness. We had not seen each other for over three months. I had cancelled the last few dinners together because of meetings to do with my film project. Perhaps she had thought I was avoiding her?

How was I? I mulled over this harmless question she had put to me. Not too bad, probably. I had felt worse. Had I felt better? If I were to draw up a scale from one to ten representing a barometer of my perceived state of mind, my mood, my physical well-being, my bodily sensations, the way I responded to my body, and if ten corresponded to that afternoon on the Amalfi coast when I remembered how, for the first time, I had sat opposite Elena in her little office at the C.N.R.S. and had inhaled her orange-tinged breath – a moment of charm, an instant of serenity that arose not from one specific and particularly happy occasion, but from a perfect balance of all the ingredients that made up my life at that time – where would I place the cursor to describe my present life? Above five, certainly, but a long way above or barely so?

I held on to the expression that we all use without ever thinking about its deeper meaning. "How are you? How is she?" I dissected it like a fruit that has suddenly become exotic without fully realising what its many rinds are concealing. I reckoned that it was comical to use a verb implying movement to characterise a mental or physical state. We see ourselves as mobile creatures. Our movement assures our happiness. If nothing moves or advances, if everything stops or comes to a standstill, the potential for happiness is extinguished and we along with it: *ça ne va plus*. We go nowhere.

For days, the city had been charged with an electrical heat that hung in the night air like the glow of a welding arc. I was stretched out on the bed, the windows open. I was smoking cigarettes in the darkness. From time to time, the passing sound of an ambulance siren broke the hollow silence outside, and then nothing more. The smell of tobacco mingled with the scent of the tall acacia trees in bloom that rose up from the inner courtyard.

Evidently, by asking me how I was, Florence wanted me to be aware that all was not well with her. We were no longer a couple, but all the same. She had remarried fairly quickly, but nevertheless. Our physical separation and our divorce had never signified the end of our relationship. It had been this way for years, in room 107 and elsewhere, in restaurants, in cafés, in conversations, in affectionate gestures, but I realised, and so did she no doubt, that in a genuinely inexplicable way Eugène's death had reshuffled the cards that we had lined up, she and I, like honest players content to be constantly replaying the same hand.

With Eugène gone, Florence also seemed to be moving away from me, or I from her, as though my friend was sweeping her off in his wake, on his journey, into the distance that his death had established. In other words, it seemed to me increasingly obvious that Florence belonged to one of my former lives, to my life with Eugène in short, that she had her central role in that existence, that existence which no longer existed.

This thought troubled me, it troubled me on her behalf, and I considered how much of what I had just discovered made me a rather unpleasant person. I knew that without ever having been truly discerning, I was getting close to the truth in this respect. And I was going to have to live with this observation, no doubt blaming myself for thinking, feeling and behaving in this way, and making myself responsible for a minor murder unknown to any police force, in which it would not be blood that flowed from the victim's body, but sorrow. Since there is no law forbidding this type of murder, I would remain unpunished.

I had a shower and sat down in front of the television. I had not switched it on for months, perhaps years. I could no longer remember the last time that I watched it. I picked up the remote control and I pressed the on-button. The screen lit up immediately. The thought occurred to me that the television was probably one of the few machines able to operate after years of inactivity and never break down, rather like the nonsense it churns out and which it feeds on, which never diminishes nor disappears.

Images appeared: a motorcycle race. The sound was at very low volume. The relentless noise of the engines was like the buzzing of insects gathering pollen. I watched the machines crammed between the thighs of the riders dressed in sadomasochistic leather suits perform a few circuits, then I switched from one channel to another at random, pressing the buttons on the remote control without even looking at them. It must have been three o'clock in the morning.

When I was about fourteen, I salvaged my aunt's black-and-white set after she had bought a colour television. I set it up in my room, opposite my bed. I spent ages there, watching the two film clubs, the one introduced by Claude-Jean Philippe on Friday evenings, and Patrick Brion's on Sunday evenings. It is to these two men that I owe most of my film buff's knowledge. Sometimes, however, due to weariness or because I found the film less enthralling, I would fall asleep and wake up later in the night: the screen was filled with a dense and distraught snowstorm that produced a slight hissing sound like that made by a pressure cooker when the steam starts to escape from it.

In those days, television separated the day from the night. Programmes stopped at about one o'clock and did not come on again until seven in the morning. Nowadays, it has broken free from the control of clocks, the biorhythms of humans, and of frontiers. With a simple flick, I moved from a discussion in Arabic between two men wearing kaffiyehs, sitting cross-legged on carpets, in what must have been a Bedouin tent, to a ballet with martial choreography performed by Chinese dancers with mechanical smiles, then to an obese Texan cook who was preparing what appeared to be a chilli con carne for the cameras, and a few seconds later I was following a seal hunter and his family who travelled about on a snowmobile over the vast whiteness.

I eventually came to a stop on an aerial shot of a very blue sea that filled the entire screen, so much so that had there not been an imperceptible and silky rolling motion that disturbed the mass of water from time to time, I would have believed they were filming a monochrome by Yves Klein.

I had switched off the sound when the American cook had begun to attack the onions violently. The image continued. It was probably a programme that was meant to make viewers feel less tense, perhaps a sequence that was part of a night-time relaxation series aimed at insomniacs, and I must admit that it worked very well as far as I was concerned. I was obsessed by the image and the soothing depths it contained. The saturation of blue, very close to the pigment of I.K.B. (International Klein Blue) and like it free of any sheen or any reflection, had the immediate effect of "absorbing" the viewer, and combined with the oily, heaving, slow rolling of the surface of the water and the circular motion of the helicopter from which the shots were filmed, acted like a tranquilliser. After a few seconds, I felt wonderfully calmed by a gentle hypnosis.

But very suddenly the picture was replaced by another shot that had nothing to do with the preceding one, even though the sea was still present, but a sea that I was unable to link to the previous one so drab and grey was it, covered with oily patches, and upon it a small boat drifted, its hull having disappeared completely apart from a mast and a section of the bows beneath a hoard of black bodies – men, women and children – all standing huddled together and staring at the lens of the camera which must have been aboard another small vessel, lighter and more mobile, to judge by the juddering image, at least twenty metres away from them.

My first reaction was not humane, I must admit – compassion

only came afterwards – but it was, let us say, of a scientific nature: how was it possible that the weight of this human cluster, which in its form and density looked like a huge swarm of bees, that you sometimes see as winter approaches, lethargic and pressed against one another, hanging from a bit of timber beneath a roof beam, or from the main branch of a tree; how was it possible that this weight did not cause the boat to sink or keel over, a boat that was virtually destroyed, barely visible and disintegrating, and looking as though it was collapsing due to the mass of wretched people?

What struck me, too, was that none of these men and women moved or spoke. They stood upright and motionless, and it was as though they were standing on the water, a weird and worrying apparition, in which they resembled creatures that were not human, endowed with supernatural powers, and whose fixed stares gave them the appearance of judges of some sort – he looked at me, they looked at us – or vigilantes, or people awaiting trial perhaps, plaintiffs who had come to hear, far out at sea, the result of a decision vital to their future.

The image eventually disappeared to be replaced by the figure of an overly made-up, auburn-haired reporter who was holding a microphone in her right hand and over her left ear wore a receiver which from time to time she was obliged to hold between the middle and index fingers of her free hand because the wind was blowing fiercely, ruffling her hair and blowing away the small piece of beige plastic that she was unable to keep in place. She was framed at chest height and was standing slightly to the left of the image so as to give viewers the opportunity to discover, in the background and to her right, a long beach, access to which, two or three metres behind the reporter, was barred by an orange plastic ribbon such as those used at crime scenes, and which gusts of wind transformed into a fluorescent serpent that seemed to be squirming in pain.

The reporter was talking. Her expression was solemn. You could sense that she was cold too, and, as she spoke, she half-turned to her left three times while continuing to look at the camera, to look at me, to point with her free hand towards what lay behind her, the expanse of the beach that stretched as far as the horizon before it was engulfed by the low sky, but along which, well before it disappeared, you could glimpse, if you looked carefully, men dressed in white uniforms similar to those worn by the staff of nuclear research establishments or investigators from the police forensic team, who were leaning over the waves and were dragging heavy, dark shapes and depositing them on the shore, while other men, dressed similarly, were laying these figures on stretchers and were walking slowly away from the sea, two by two, carrying these stretchers now made heavier by the weight of the lifeless bodies towards some small vans, lined up at an angle one beside the other.

Groping around, I searched for the remote control while keeping my eyes firmly fixed on the screen and, at the moment that I felt it in the palm of my hand and very quickly found the sound button to turn off the "silent" mode, the screen was once again entirely filled with the image of the sea that had soothed me so much a few minutes earlier, and a female voice, probably that of the reporter, provided a caption to this image, giving it an acoustic counterpoint, frantic and provoking anxiety, even though she was speaking Italian which is the language in which, because of its musicality, the worst horrors and incompetence can sound charming, explaining, from what I was able to understand, that there, at this spot that the helicopter was flying over, in this marvellously flat, ultramarine expanse, silky and eternal, a few sea miles from Lampedusa, a small vessel that did not deserve the name cargo boat had sunk, carrying down to the depths of the Mediterranean – which the reporter, on two occasions, as though to emphasise the irony of the expression, referred to by its ancient name of *mare nostrum* – eight hundred migrants who had fled a Libya ravaged by war, and of whom only a few bodies had later been thrown up on the coast.

XX

I WAS UNABLE TO GET TO SLEEP. MY INSOMNIA WAS, OF course, ridiculous. I was not expecting to revive the dead because of it, nor pay my share in the human tragedy. But I was not going to allow myself to slip away into a soothing slumber when so many other men had died in dramatic conditions, without anybody offering them a helping hand.

What I had seen had, in many ways, profoundly shocked me. I had succumbed to the lure of the beauty of the sea, which I had taken at face value, without realising that what I was being shown was at the very same time the instrument that had caused a massive number of deaths, and an impassive graveyard. This misjudgement made an impotent ass of me, sprawled comfortably on a sofa. But I also questioned myself about the sequence of shots, about the editing of the report that the director of the Italian channel had chosen to broadcast. One could sense the influence of cinema in the emission, of fiction, or rather the dramatic tension associated with certain fictional films. And this haunted me too, as though, somewhere, through my own work, which had had nothing to do *a priori* with this, I shared a degree of responsibility, perhaps not directly in what had happened, but nonetheless in the manner in which it had been shown.

I remembered the perfect equilibrium of the opening of one of Roman Polanski's films, "The Ghost Writer". At the very beginning, at nightfall, we see a ferry arriving at a port, docking there, and the cars and the passengers disembarking. The second shot shows the hold of the ferry, all vehicles removed apart from one, which the owner has not collected and which a breakdown lorry is about to tow away. In the third shot, filmed at night, we see police officers examining the vehicle which has been unloaded onto the quayside. Finally, the fourth shot, in daylight, reveals a wild beach battered by waves, and suddenly, within these waves, we can make out the shape of a body which the sea rolls over and eventually deposits on the shore.

This was the kind of textbook that the director of the Italian channel had followed. The real tragedy had not been enough. He or she had found it necessary, through focusing, through the merits and chosen sequence of selected shots, to portray the scene so as to intensify the horror and probably make it more accessible to viewers who cannot see the world nowadays and be moved or touched by it without the coded schedules that fictional images have suggested to them over the decades and that have shaped their brains and their sensibilities.

By a sort of reverse shock, fiction shapes the universe. The film world, with its codes, its rules and its archetypes, influences those men and women who produce images of reality. One only has to see how members of criminal, pseudo-religious Middle Eastern organisations film and subsequently produce beheadings of hostages to realise that it is from Hollywood and the West, which they nevertheless regard as the repository of values they despise and fight against, that they borrow their language. What is more, their power to provoke terror is entirely dependent upon the image, for the murders they continue to commit would only have a limited effect if there were no sites or networks to show their videos. The responsibility of servers such as YouTube, Dailymotion and many others is therefore immense, for by agreeing to show such images, they are instantly equipping them with a power that is immeasurable, and through them they are guaranteeing power to the people who make them.

Dawn was beginning to tint the roofs of Paris in a pink wash. Through my window, I looked out on Elena's apartment and in her room, on the bed, I could visualise the shape of her vulnerable body and that of her hair, which sleep had spread-eagled into a fan. It was not the sea that was covering her, it was simply the night, the night which was beginning to withdraw, as though summoned elsewhere, on the other side of the world, by the oscillating force of celestial tides. I thought of all those legends, which I had read ever since childhood, about creatures living beneath the seas, in crystal palaces, about beautiful, fluid sirens, slipping through the currents, mingling tears shed by inconsolable, forsaken creatures in the briny depths; I thought of Jules Supervielle's stories in *Enfant de la haute* mer, of the wails of drowning sailors, of Pierre MacOrlan's *Roi rose* and all the ghost ships.

The earth, the blue planet, then seemed to me to be blue from pain, a huge swollen entity covered in bruises, continually devouring thousands of bodies, in its oceans, its earthquakes, its avalanches, its mud-flows and its landslips, its belligerent follies, its cyclones and tempests, like a terrifyingly primitive and placid creature that demands its daily ration of fresh flesh in order to continue being what it is, a beautiful round and apathetic body that tolerates our dwelling on its back provided that we do not irritate it too much.

The bells of Saint-Sulpice began to peal out. The beat of bronze hammers on the bulky structures caused the windows on either side of the bar to vibrate, as well as the small table at which Florence and I were sitting. The surface of the coffee I had not drunk rippled with concentric circles that reminded me of the turbulence of a pond after you throw a stone into it. I thought again suddenly of the drowned people of Lampedusa.

"Why did you call me, me of all people, to tell me this?" Florence then asked me. "You have other ears to listen to you nowadays, don't you?"

I left Lampedusa and I gazed at her. Her lovely face was like a sky over which I had seen time, the days and the nights, the rainstorms and the sunshine – my life – pass.

"I was lost."

She thought for a while, weighing up the words she was about to utter, hesitating whether to say them to me, perhaps. The bells had ceased chiming.

"And when you're lost, it's up to me to find you again, is that it?"

XXI

THE SHAPE OF OUR LIVES IS NOT AT ALL LINEAR. IT IS more like the only copy of a book, which for some of us consists of just a few pages, clean and smooth, covered in sensible, careful handwriting, while for others there is a much more substantial number of loose leaves, some of them torn, others more or less deleted, and full of repetitions and *retouches*. Each page corresponds to a moment of our existence and particularly to the person we were at that time, and are no longer, and whom we look at, if ever we feel the desire or need to leaf through the book, as both strange and paradoxically strangely familiar.

I was tempted to raise this observation with Michel Piccoli. Perhaps because the actor's age and his sweetness of manner, and the kindliness of his gaze – a gaze that is not piercing, but broad and soft, and as though blurred at the edges – made me think that he might be able to understand me. Eugène knew Michel Piccoli from having produced a film twenty or so years ago in which Michel played the main role. I had glimpsed the actor at my friend's burial, walking slowly, stooped and gentle, and looking as though he were lost in the crowd like a child at a party for grown-ups. At the time, I was only beginning to think about what would eventually become the subject of "*La Fabrique intérieure*", and it was only later, when I heard the actor's voice on France Culture, in a series of radio interviews on the programme "*À voix nue*", which was devoted to him, that it seemed to me obvious and essential that it should be he who would play the part of Écho 23 987, the man-made creature delivered to Paul, the character in my film.

When I got in touch with him through his agent, Michel Piccoli replied to me straight away, suggesting a meeting not in some luxury bar, as is often the case with actors and actresses who pretend to like privacy yet who first and foremost enjoy being recognised, but in a McDonald's near his home, explaining to me when I met him that at least we would not be disturbed here since none of this clientele made up of young people knew who he was:

"I belong to an era that is past. Like dinosaurs and good manners."

At first, we talked about Eugène whom he told me in solemn and affectionate tones he liked very much. And he repeated this simple sentence "I liked him very much" three times, which might have been simply politeness had not the resonance of his voice, his slowness, his dreamy sagacity, and the faraway smile on his face bestowed on him, without any shadow of doubt, the stamp of truthfulness.

When I began to describe "*La Fabrique intérieure*" and suggested that I leave with him the script I had brought so that he could have time to read it, he stopped me and asked me to tell him the story, informing me that scripts bored him, that when reading them one never knew the importance the director attached to them, that one didn't know whether the guy was ready to die for his work, or whether he simply wanted to show off with a camera so that he could appear on two or three television programmes and be taken seriously.

He had said this to me without wishing to be provocative, but as a sort of observation acquired in the course of a very long career. He had also been keen to point out that he was not very familiar with my work, apart from a documentary that I had made about an old man, a skilled watchmaker, and another film that took place entirely in a forest – my second film, "*Après*" – which followed the wanderings and attempts to survive of a man played by Benoît Régent, whom we assume to be a deserter who has fled from a war, neither the name nor the date of which is ever made clear.

I began at the beginning. I told him about Elena whom I had seen from my window, some way away, simply a body walking around against a background viewed from a distance, who seemed to be waiting for me to provide her with a story, a character, feelings, memories; for me to bring her to life, to place her in situations that I would imagine for her, to integrate her gradually into my life and to make a real person of her.

Piccoli listened to me carefully, occasionally sipping – evidently with great pleasure – with a straw from his strawberry milkshake, while my "royal bacon" and chips, which I had ordered because one had to order something, but which I had not touched, grew cold in front of me. All around us, young black teenagers were listening to rap music played through the loudspeakers of their mobile phones, their heads nodding like plaster cherubs in churches, who only have to be fed with a coin to activate them. They spoke in loud voices, as if they were deaf or as if the volume of their voices was stuck at maximum.

My intention was not to make a science-fiction film in the conventional sense of the term. The future that it examined was sufficiently contemporary for the scenery, the clothing and the habitual practices to be no different from those we are familiar with today. The fable that I wished to construct would be performed with a certain fantasy, which would basically depend on the relationship those who owned an Echo would maintain with their creatures, making them into robots endowed with minimal powers and knowledge, or on the contrary, machines that specialised in a field of extreme precision.

The fact that the majority of buyers opt for models that look young and are equipped with fine physiques would immediately create a double problem: they would be participating in a standard-isation of the personal landscape – the same male and female types, young and good-looking, would suddenly be over-represented and this over-representation would simultaneously lead to depressive behaviour among human beings, incapable as far as their incor-ruptible creation was concerned of accepting their own lack of elegance and the ageing of their bodies.

The case of Paul, who chooses to order and own a rather unconventional Echo and insists that it should have the features of an old man, worries the government department, but there is no law that can prevent the company that manufactures the robots from agreeing to his request.

When it is discovered that unlike his fellow citizens, he is not content with inserting a few bits of basic data and some memories into his Echo, but is spending his days and nights running memory circuits that are available throughout the internet in order to feed into his creature not merely all the world's memory and all known knowledge, but also behavioural and psychological aspects that cover every situation that a human being may encounter during its life, the State decides to remove his robot and destroy it.

But how can anyone destroy what surpasses everything that is known in knowledge and intelligence? Écho 23 987 is not simply made up of the equivalent of all the data available on the web; it also possesses, through its ability to combine and its capacity for unlimited expansion of its own sharp memory, a few nanoseconds' lead over its networks. Écho 23 987 surpasses all other machines, envelops them and makes them obsolete.

Basically, it is nothing but an ultra-powerful computer, capable of extending these powers in real time, but what seems to be intolerable to those who govern is that it should have outwardly human features, the appearance of a dreamy and gentle old man. It is as though God were suddenly to manifest Himself when, for centuries, human beings have never stopped wanting to be free of Him and to kill Him. And it is very much this symbolic aspect that becomes unacceptable. Why should it matter if this body be made up of a synthetic skin concealing printed circuits and storage centres: its appearance is too human and its powers too inhuman. This signs its death warrant, but the film is open-ended: how does one manage to make something that is not alive die?

When I stopped talking, I felt as though I was a candidate who has just taken an important exam and is waiting restlessly for the verdict of the examiner who is sitting opposite him. Michel Piccoli was in no rush to break the silence. He studied me carefully, as though he was trying to decipher from my expression what I was ultimately trying to keep to myself, then he glanced down at the table and, pointing to the small round packet wrapped in grease-proof paper, asked me:

"Aren't you going to eat your hamburger?"

And without waiting for me to answer, he grabbed the bun, unwrapped it, and bit into my "royal bacon", chewing a mouthful and wincing.

"It's rather squalid of me, but I can't bear food being wasted. I'm a war baby, you see."

Not quite sure how to react, I must have assented, wondering whether he was making fun of me or whether he had suddenly gone crazy. But before taking a second bite, he continued:

"I've never played God. A pope, yes, but not God. I've been waiting for this for ages!"

And he laughed, he laughed very loudly, he laughed so loudly that all of a sudden the music and conversation in the place stopped. Simultaneously. At the same second.

XXII

I HAVE NEVER LIKED VISITING RUINS. I KNOW ONLY too well that I am insignificant, but the haughty architects of bygone centuries remind me of the fact too fiercely and too grandly. As much as anyone else, I need a little illusion to carry on.

It is early July and the heat is unremitting. I search for shade beneath the arches of the great amphitheatre at Pula, but there is little to be had, and in every protected nook and cranny I find a few worn-out tourists sitting on the ground, who look at me without a shred of kindliness, ready to argue aggressively and with the weapons at their disposal – cameras with outsize lenses, flasks, walking sticks, iPhones for the territory they have acquired.

Elena goes out in the full sunlight. It's as though she feels the heat less, as though the sun is sparing her and merely tanning her. She is happy to be here, and I am happy that she is happy. She tells me about the places where she came to play as a child, the goats and sheep that used to graze there, between the blocks of stone, in what was then a shapeless arena and where the grass seemed greener than elsewhere. Elena is nimble. Elena is beautiful. Elena is young.

I spin out these sentences like propositions in a theorem, but I reach no conclusion. I've never been any good at maths.

We have been here for four days. The city is not very big. It's not very beautiful either. Or rather, it's no longer very beautiful. It's a patched-up sort of creature, an organism made up of various limbs and which hang together as best they can: the Graeco-Roman remains, the Austro-Hungarian Empire, Communism, Ultra-Liberal anarchy, the land with its olive trees, the sea with its unattractive beaches, and the shipyards.

Elena drags me into the churches, which are cool and unpretentious. I discover that she is devout. She lights candles, she crosses herself and seems to be murmuring prayers. I leave her to it, and look at the paintings, the paving, and the walls with their cracked plaster that look like incomplete topographical surveys criss-crossed by meandering rivers.

"Are you a believer?"

She smiles at me and does not reply. She takes my arm, kisses me. Still that orange scent.

I go into ecstasies at coming across a public urinal, a *pissotière*. I try to share my delight with Elena.

"Do you realise, a real *pissotière*, where one can still piss!"

"You men can, not us women."

"Free, always open! There's not a single one like this left in France."

"So much the better!"

I step inside the decorated tin-plate oval construction. Everything is here, the powerful stench which many, including Elena, find appalling, the obscene graffiti, the flies, the trickle of rusty water that attempts unsuccessfully to steer urine and paper towards an open hole that resembles the eye of a large toad. I pee. And while I am peeing I can see outside, because my face is level with a slit cut into the structure. Elena is sitting on a bench ten yards away.

"I can see you!"

"I can see you too."

She turns around and looks at the sea, an inlet of the sea, with an island in the distance. Ships sail by, small trawlers. Men on the bridge call out to one another as they gather in the nets. I leave the *pissotière*. I return to Elena.

"I used to come and sit on this bench with my mother and father. I never stayed long on it. In summer, I would play on the grass. There were other children. In winter, or when the weather was bad, I stayed in the alleyways. There were fewer children. My parents didn't leave the bench. My mother took out a magazine, my father his cigarettes. He just smoked as he gazed at the sea. They didn't talk to one another. My father didn't converse with the other men who greeted him as they passed. He smoked and gazed at the sea. He always seemed a bit melancholy when we came here. And in the evening, his melancholy persisted. He remained sitting at his place in the kitchen, he continued to gaze ahead of him, slightly into the distance, as though the sea were there, concealed in the patterns of the wallpaper which depicted multicoloured birds and monkeys. Normally, he was cheerful and sang songs all the time, or he whistled. But the sea made him feel sad, and yet we would often go and sit beside it. When we left Pula to come and live in France, there was no longer any sea, but he never sang or whistled again. Sadness swept over him. It overcame him. I think he had left lots of doors open. He was waiting for some illness or other to enter and take root in him. It was sadness. He died of it. Very quickly. He was thirty-eight years old and I was twelve."

The olive oil here is a wild green colour. It has a fiery taste and a bitterness that I enjoy. I dip chunks of bread into my plate and it looks like those Turkish breads that Florence and I used to eat our fill of on our first trips together. Florence.

Florence has suddenly invited herself to our table at this little restaurant near the main square of Pula, with its low ceiling and its pitifully conventional decor – flasks of wine and fishing nets hanging from the walls. All I had to do was bite into the bread to be reminded of her. I don't know what she would make of that. Whether she would laugh or give me a slap.

My body has more of a memory than I do. The taste of Turkish bread. Florence. Malatya. The burning wind on the summit of Nemrut Dagi. The apricot trees and our youthfulness. "Bring me back some tobacco," Eugène had asked. We had brought him back some tobacco, bought by weight in the souk at Diyarbakir which had been set up in the ancient *caravanserai*. Men seated on the ground were selling a honey-coloured and fragrant-smelling tobacco that was piled in large pyramids on open sheets in front of them. Outside, in daylight that was so bright that the sky was neither blue nor white but unbearably steely, the temperature was over forty degrees. At night, we took cold showers every two hours and we got back into bed soaked, hoping to retain the coolness of the water on our naked flesh. In the morning, we had oranges, biscuits and tea for breakfast.

Three weeks ago, I had dinner with Florence, before her departure. It was she who had suggested dinner. Perhaps it was her going away as well, but the pretext was her husband Luc's transfer. It's strange for me to be writing "her husband" when referring to Florence, and that it should no longer be me. Luc has an important position in a multinational company that deals with the recycling of household waste. When, a few years ago, Florence had told me what his job was, it had made me laugh: "So he's taking care of me," I had said to her. She had not reacted. She had shrugged her shoulders, taken the bottle of Sancerre from the bucket and poured some for both of us. Florence complained about never seeing me. I don't know whether she sees more of Luc. But perhaps that suits her.

"Luc has been appointed to a post in Brazil. In São Paulo."

I had tried to recall São Paulo, where I had been to a festival some time ago. I remembered arriving by helicopter on the roof of a hotel; the climate, which I had been mistaken about – I had only brought summer clothes and the temperature was thirteen degrees; I remembered a cultural attaché who had pretty pear-shaped breasts that I could make out beneath her beige crêpe blouse; a vast city, dreary and impassive; a cigar, I think it was a Magnum 46, smoked on the terrace of a Starbucks as I watched people go by;

the hours spent in cars in order to reach one part of the city from another; a fairly short discussion after the film; an exhibition of Sebastião Salgado's photographs that took place in a cultural site located inside a sports complex where an Olympic swimming pool had been built below ground, so that when you walked through the exhibition rooms, you were walking over glass paving beneath which, ten metres or so below, you could see swimmers moving to and fro; another exhibition of drawings by Lucian Freud, fleshy and convoluted; the pink face of a T.A.M. stewardess on my flight home who showed a slightly worrying concern for my well-being and security, adjusting my seat belt and pulling my rug up to my neck as though I were five years old.

"São Paolo's wonderful," was all I replied.

We had finished our dinner and were exchanging trivial remarks, as I assume men and women do when they meet for the first time, through a personal ad, and realise that they are not suited to one another, but who decide nevertheless to remain polite and friendly during the rest of the meal.

It was only once I had closed the door of Florence's taxi that I became aware that I might be seeing her for the last time in my life, that an ocean would now divide us, that time zones would play havoc with the arrangements we had shared up till then, that I could never again tell myself we were breathing the same air, were living in the same city, were getting up with the same sunrise. I know her well enough, I know her too well, not to realise that she would be having the same thoughts as me at that moment, and that like me she probably only wanted one thing, for someone somewhere to stop time's pendulum, for me to open the taxi door again, for me to offer her my hand, for her to take it, get out of the cab and come and snuggle up in my arms never to leave them again.

But taxi drivers do their job, which is to drive cabs, to set off once the passenger is inside, without worrying about their state of mind or their dithering.

This is the way our lives go, when decisions are sometimes made a little too quickly, and we are left afterwards untangling our regrets and our guilt.

Elena is looking at me.

"Are you dreaming?" she asks me.

"No," I reply, "I'm simply remembering." She has the tact or the absent-mindedness not to ask me what about. I think I love her all the more for that.

The following morning, a warm drizzle descends on Pula. Mysteriously, Elena wants to take me somewhere, at all costs. I am dragging my leg a little, rather like a worn-out old nag. We have an early breakfast and leave the hotel like conspirators. It's a Sunday. The streets are deserted. We walk hand in hand up a long avenue lined with ancient barrack buildings, in which I imagine entire garrisons waiting to embark aboard gleaming battleships at anchor in the harbour. The First World War is at its height. Pula is the only outlet to the sea in the whole of the Austro-Hungarian Empire. Neither its leader nor his subjects realise that they are living out their last moments, and that soon the world will collapse, that soon their vast territory will become a huge area of bleeding flesh that will be partitioned off.

Elena is ahead of me now, walking quickly. She leads the way, turning around from time to time to encourage me with a smile. I fondled her breasts at dawn and laid my face between her thighs to breathe in her smell and her life. I sense that she is different this morning and is keeping herself to herself.

At the end of the long avenue in which we have encountered no-one, apart from three mangy dogs and, further on, much higher up, an old man wearing a baseball cap and mumbling incomprehensible recriminations into his beard, we enter an area of abandoned villages.

These are houses of an inhuman size, built for a defunct nobility who used to come there, a century ago, in the sea-bathing season, bringing with them in their carriages an army of servants, nannies, tutors, cooks, English governesses and chauffeurs. All of them are in a state of decay which merely serves to emphasise, by default, the splendour that was once theirs.

Often, you can see that much later on, toward the mid-century, at a time when people dreamed of a collective life, they were crudely partitioned into flats and were neglected rather like traitors being punished. Their roofs are crumbling here and there. Breezeblocks of cement fill some of the windows. The balconies are collapsing. In the greenhouse and winter gardens, bits of wrecked cars are rusting. Their gardens are nothing but unsightly jungles overgrown with broom and invaded by wildcats, or mournful expanses, untended and muddy, over which the fine Croatian rain falls like a broth, among the detritus, the plastic buckets, the broken toys of children who have now grown up, become forgetful teenagers and later adults with no memories. The plaster is crumbling into flaky patches. The timber structures are spewing out brown liquid. Smashed roof tiles on the ground resemble playing cards that had been left there, after games had ended without there being any winner. Yet occasionally, some wisteria, a camellia, a clump of elderly rhododendrons looking like pomegranate trees still testify to some former elegance.

Elena has taken my hand again and I let her lead me. We stop at the corner of two streets, in front of a low brick wall through which an iron gate gives on to a pathway of scattered stones. It leads to the tradesman's entrance to one of the villas where you can only see the hump-shaped rear section, designed to look like the half-timbered houses in Normandy built of wattle and daub. The lord of the manor who had approved the construction had no doubt wished to be reminded of his summers spent in Trouville, of all the money tossed onto the green baize cloths of the casinos at Deauville and Yvetot, and the early mornings after the gambling and the champagne, passed between silken sheets, in the arms of a slightly buxom courtesan who whispered words of love and obscenities to him in French.

A fearful sadness oozes from the walls of this fragment of France, half-strangled by the vegetation consisting of elder, purple hazelnut bushes, honeysuckle that has reverted to the wild, and the branches of a maritime pine that no one has dared to prune. But unlike the other houses, this one still retains a soul, even though the soul is wounded.

Elena draws my attention to two windows on the top floor. Their woodwork is painted in almond green and the narrow embroidered curtains, which fail to cover the full width of each casement, hang over the windowpanes like church linen cloths. On the shutter of one of them, a cuttlefish bone has been hung for the birds. Quarrelsome sparrows are busy pecking at it.

"That's where . . ." she says to me. "That's where I spent my childhood."

I know what places can mean. I know how much they shape us and how they can leave marks that haunt us like scars. I imagine Elena as a little girl, hanging a fresh cuttlefish from the hook on the shutter, and the voice of her mother, perhaps, telling her to be careful, not to lean out, to come back quickly and to close the window.

Elena has snuggled up to me and has laid her cheek on my shoulder. I stroke her hair and we both look up at the windows which, behind the patter of the drizzle, enclose for ever the happy times, the sorrows and the hope-filled slumbers of a little girl who is no longer there. At that moment I feel myself caught up in a circular slow-motion, a dizziness that leaves me feeling anxious as when, like a lost traveller, you are not sure when the crossroads will finally come into view, which road embodies an unknown promise, and which other one would lead us to a land that is all too familiar.

Without my being aware, Elena has slipped from my grasp and is now standing in front of me. She is gazing at me and smiling. It is a smile I don't recognise and it seeps into me, dispersing a radiant warmth, fertile and overflowing, throughout my body. We stare at one another for a long time. Elena fills me with her smile, her tranquillity, the breath that swells in her breast. It's a scene from the movies, of course. It can only be a scene from the movies. A scene that exists purely in films and all of a sudden I no longer know whether I am experiencing it or whether I am watching it in the reassuring darkness of a cinema.

"I'm expecting a baby. Your baby."

Have I dreamed what Elena has just said to me? Is someone about to switch on the lights, or leave me in this uncertain country for a little while longer, for a moment, a very brief moment?

"A baby," she repeats, pointing to her belly.

Is it the rain that is speaking or Elena's voice?

Have the windows up above opened, or is it a dream perhaps; a girl has appeared and is looking at us?

"I wanted to tell you this, here. Here in the land where I grew up."

And Elena takes my hand, solemnly, and places it on her belly.

XXIII

IT IS NOVEMBER 2, THE DAY OF THE DEAD IN THE Christian tradition. At the cemetery that stood opposite the house where I grew up, on the other side of the road, it was the most beautiful and the liveliest day of the year. The flowers laid on the graves and the constant comings and goings of families in their Sunday best transformed it into a colourful park in which people walked, where the surrounding area was thronged with cars and from which all sadness and all distress seemed to have been cast out.

In about an hour's time the first day of filming of "*La Fabrique intérieure*" begins. In front of me, Eugène is still sitting at the terrace of his café and is looking into the distance, to his right, with a calm half-smile on his face. He hasn't aged in the slightest. This morning, I should like him to turn his head towards me, for once, so that I can look him in the eye and say to him: there you are, you see, you would be happy, you would be proud, it's all beginning again, I've pulled myself together, you're not there but I'm carrying on as I promised you I would.

Above the noise and the sounds of footsteps and the clanging, and voices in which I recognise only murmurs and quavers, I can hear some joyful and well-organised urgency. My team is putting the last touches to the preparations for the main location, which is Paul's apartment. I have chosen Éric Ruf to play the part of Paul. For a long time I have been fascinated by this Comédie-Française actor, who used to perform there, staged plays there, and now runs the theatre. With his intense and driven physique, he reminds me from certain angles of Antonin Artaud in Abel Gance's "Napoléon". I don't know him well. He is shy and reserved. When I brought them together for the first time, Michel Piccoli and he looked at each other for a long time, without speaking, without being able to speak, and such was the human depth in that first silent interaction, I regretted not having brought a camera with me. Éric is already on the set.

At my request, Kim Soo rented for the set the apartment that belonged to Monsieur Bellagar, my old neighbour from the eighth floor, whom I spotted one morning when he was moving house on the pavement outside my building. He was waiting for the removal van to be loaded, sitting on a kitchen chair beside his piano. He doffed his hat when I greeted him. We smiled at one another. It was only at that moment that I realised we had never exchanged a single word. I told myself that it was a bit late to start. Was I wrong perhaps?

Behind me, as I write these final lines, Michel Piccoli is sitting on one of the sofas. He is waiting, wrapped in a white towelling dressing gown like a boxer retaining his muscle heat before he climbs into the ring. I was getting ready to film him naked, when Paul, having unwrapped the packaging from around the robotic creature that has just been delivered to him, discovers that it doesn't move and is not wearing any clothing.

The camera is going to make a slow tracking spiral over his octogenarian's body. Michel knows this. He has agreed to it. He understands that the shot should delineate the appearance of a body that has been affected by age and coalesces with the limited length of human life, and that beyond it, perhaps, beyond the wonderfully weary skin, the muscles and the worn-out bones, and the distended flesh, the domain of God may possibly begin.

At that moment, I imagine him leafing through one of the books on the low table, among them one that I deliberately left there so that it could not be missed, about the sculptor Ligier Richier whose work "*Le Transi*" in the church of Saint-Étienne in Bar-le-Duc features a dead man who we see standing, still partially resembling a living person, with flesh, hair and tendons, clearly reminding us of what we once were and what we will become, and whose lost body, heaped together in the delicacy of the hollowed-out marble by the artist, testifies both to our death and to the love of those who live on after us, and thanks to whom we survive, for the work was commissioned by the woman whose husband, René de Chalon, Prince of Orange, comrade in arms of Charles V, had just been killed in a battle beneath the ramparts of Saint-Dizier in 1544. This very young widow asked the sculptor to represent her lost and beloved one as he might look after three years spent in his tomb, beneath the cold earth of Lorraine. And at that moment some lines came back to me, I don't remember whether they are from Ovid or Epicurus, or whether I dreamed them, just as I sometimes dream of dialogue, of snatches of conversation, titles of books or scenes from films: "My body, old friend, so has the time come for us to take our leave of one another?"

But perhaps the actor who is getting ready to play the part of this robotic god into whom all the world's memory – its complexities, its inconsistencies and its hopes – is to be poured, is looking instead at Elena who, reclining on the sofa in the flat opposite, as she likes to do, is stretching out her long legs on the Indonesian cushions, decorated with gold threads and wood fibres, which I brought back from the land of the Toraja, and is watching me at my table, busy writing these final lines before laying aside the computer and words in a few minutes to become just a minor image maker.

So what is she thinking about as she watches me like this from behind, outlined against the window, against the November sky in which clouds flit by, pregnant with the rains they are keeping for other landscapes?

I imagine her with both hands resting on her belly that is beginning to fill out, searching beneath her palm for the movements inside her, slow and sometimes spasmodic, of the little creature that is still sleeping, its eyes closed, floating in a sort of weightlessness within a dark and warm liquid, innocent of all memory, of all emotion, of all sorrow, and in which the miraculous conjunction of life has bonded our two distinct selves.

It now seems to me that I shall never be any other age but this baby's, and that forgetting my body, forgetting who I am, forgetting my troubles and my doubts, my mistakes, my wounds, I shall belong entirely to that child, in order that he or she may live, love, laugh, marvel and grow as tall as the heavens.

Author's note

AT THE BEGINNING OF OCTOBER 2015, AS I WAS reading through the proofs of this book, I learned of the accidental death of Isabelle Collignon, who was a bookseller in Chamonix. I was deeply moved by this news. Isabelle loved her family and friends. She loved life, her beautiful valley and her mountains, the literature that she constantly stood up for. She was not able to read *The Tree of the Toraja*, as I would have wished, but by way of affectionate homage I should like her, whose sweet and unfailing smile I shall remember, to be welcomed into its pages.

PHILIPPE CLAUDEL

PHILIPPE CLAUDEL is a university lecturer, novelist, film director and scriptwriter. He has written fourteen novels that have been translated into various languages. In 2009 his film "I've Loved You So Long", which draws upon Claudel's eleven years teaching in prisons, won the BAFTA for Best Foreign Language film. Among his novels, *Grey Souls* won the Prix Renaudot in France, the American Gumshoe Award and the Swedish Martin Beck award. *Brodeck's Report* won the 2010 *Independent* Foreign Fiction Award.

EUAN CAMERON's translations from French include *Monsieur Linh and His Child* and *Parfums* by Philippe Claudel, works by Julien Green, Simone de Beauvoir, Paul Morand and Patrick Modiano, as well as biographies of Marcel Proust and Irène Némirovsky.

A New Library from MacLehose Press

This book is part of a new international library for literature in translation. MacLehose Press has become known for its wide-ranging list of bestselling European crime writers, eclectic non-fiction and winners of the Nobel and *Independent* Foreign Fiction prizes, and for the many awards given to our translators. In their own countries, our writers are celebrated as the very best.

Join us on our journey to **READ THE WORLD**.

www.maclehosepress.com